The Billionaire Playboy

The Sherbrookes of Newport

Christina Tetreault

The Billionaire Playboy, Copyright 2012 by Christina Tetreault

Published by Christina Tetreault

DIGITAL ISBN: 978-0-9883089-0-9
PRINT ISBN: 978-0-9883089-1-6

OTHER BOOKS BY CHRISTINA

CHAPTER 1

I sure picked a hell of a time to come home. Charlotte O'Brien, or Charlie as her friends called her, sat in the darkened living room of her family's bed and breakfast, The Victorian Rose. Outside, Hurricane Andrea raged with gale force winds exceeding 110 miles per hour. As expected the hurricane arrived in the northeastern part of Massachusetts in the early morning hours. While it was not the first hurricane she had experienced in her life, it was the fiercest she could remember.

She could hear the howling winds outside as they caused the branches from nearby trees to slam into the side of the house. A constant deluge of rain pelted the windows, which rattled from time to time under the onslaught. Frequently she'd see debris fly by the window. The most recent object looked like siding from a nearby house. So far her family and their home remained unscathed, but what about the rest of the town? Charlie reached for the battery-powered radio and switched it on. After several tries she got a local AM station to come in. The faceless voice of the radio announcer filled the silent room. "Severe flooding is already being seen on Church Street."

1

This announcement came as no big surprise. It had poured almost every day the previous week and the waterlogged ground and swollen rivers couldn't accommodate this new round of rain.

The sound of shattering glass, followed by a crash, filled the room and blocked out anything else the radio announcer may have said. Without a second thought Charlie jumped to her feet and yanked her mother off the couch in front of the windows and pushed her toward a chair in the corner. At the same instant her brother Sean burst into the room.

"A tree just went through the dining room window. Take Ma into the basement." After giving his order Sean disappeared upstairs, his huge Irish Wolfhound, Max, following at his heels. She hated to admit it, but she should have thought of that sooner. The basement was the safest place during a hurricane.

"Come on Ma, let's go." Charlie grabbed the battery-powered radio and flashlight next to her and stood.

"What about Sean?" Maureen O'Brien sat perched on the edge of a chair, her face pale and her hands gripping the arms of the chair.

For half a heartbeat anger and resentment surged through Charlie. Why couldn't the woman ever do anything she asked? It was always about Sean. Almost as soon as the emotions came on they disappeared. Circumstances outside everyone's control had created a much tighter relationship between her mother and older brother. It wasn't fair to either of them to resent it—it wasn't as if her mother didn't love her. Sean was her mother's rock and had been since that day seventeen years earlier when her dad walked out on them. That day Sean became the man of the house. "Sean wants us downstairs now. He'll be down soon."

With some reluctance Maureen came to her feet and, as usual, Charlie felt like a giant standing next to her mother. At five feet eight inches she towered over her mother who barely reached five feet. Despite the height difference there was no mistaking them for mother and daughter. Both had thick red hair, and hazel eyes that seemed to change colors depending on their mood.

Using her flashlight, Charlie led her mom through the dark house toward the basement door, a door she could have found even without the bright beam of light. Having grown up in the old Victorian she knew every nook and cranny of the house. Without even thinking she instinctively flipped the light switch then felt like an idiot when nothing happened.

"Be careful," Charlie said over her shoulder as she started down the steep wooden stairs.

The beam from her flashlight bounced off the rock walls as the familiar scent of the basement enveloped her. She hadn't stepped foot in the basement in years, yet she would have recognized the smell anywhere. Since the basement remained remarkably dry her mom hung fresh herbs down there making it constantly smell like basil and rosemary. Some things just never changed.

Behind her she heard the bottom step creak, as it had for years, letting her know that her mother had safely made it down the stairs.

"I hope everything is all right out there."

Was her mom serious? A hurricane raged outside. Though a smart reply was on the tip of her tongue, Charlie held it back. When her mom was upset she had a tendency to ignore the obvious. So instead of saying anything she headed over to a partitioned-off section of the basement where her brother kept his pool table and several folding chairs.

After taking down the battery-powered lantern on the shelf and turning it on, Charlie sat in one of the stiff plastic folding chairs and listened to the news reports coming over the radio.

"Reports are coming in that the Stonefield Dam shows signs of giving out. Anyone living near the dam or along the river should leave the area immediately." The faceless voice came through the radio, causing a ball of dread to form in the pit of Charlie's stomach. The area around the river and dam was heavily populated. If the dam let go a lot of people could be hurt. Unfortunately, there wasn't a thing she could do about it. Instead of focusing on what she couldn't control, Charlie thought about the things she could. Right now that meant keeping her mom safe and calm until the storm passed.

"I noticed that you repainted the living room. It looks nice." Idle chatter would help her mom pass the time and focus on something other than the hurricane and Sean's absence. Drumming her fingers on her leg she waited in the semi-darkness for her mom to answer.

"It hadn't been done in a long time. Sean thought it was a good idea," Maureen replied as the sound of heavy footsteps coming down the stairs alerted them to Sean's arrival.

Before Charlie could comment further all six feet three inches of her brother appeared along with his giant dog. Immediately the smell of wet dog assaulted her senses. No wonder it had taken Sean so long to get down there. He'd gone outside. What had he been thinking?

"You two okay? The big maple near the shed just went down. The roots were ripped right out of the ground." Sean pulled a chair next to Charlie's.

***

Charlie blew a strand of hair which had escaped from her bun out of her face and rolled her shoulders. Sweat trickled down her back causing her t-shirt to stick to her skin. More than anything she wanted a hot shower to wash away the grime and sweat covering her body.

Since early morning she'd been systematically going through town with the other volunteers checking on its citizens and assessing the damage. It wasn't a pretty sight. The once picture-perfect New England town looked as if a Navy bomber had dropped a missile on North Salem,

Massachusetts. The most severe damage was down by the river where the dam once stood. The entire area now sat under several feet of water. Charlie and several others were slowly working their way to that end of the town. Toppled trees and downed power lines made the trip slow and dangerous. On the positive side though, there had been very few serious injuries reported. Most of the ones she'd seen or heard about involved gashes from breaking glass and thrown-out backs from moving tree limbs and other debris. With any luck it would stay that way.

Rolling her shoulders Charlie looked around at the other volunteers. Many of them leaned against trees or sat on the rain-drenched ground oblivious to the mud as they took a much-deserved break. Like her, most had started working hours earlier, the minute the storm passed. Despite the fatigue clawing at her body, Charlie didn't join the others. She needed to keep working. When there was work to do, she couldn't rest. After taking a long drink of water, she tossed the bottle back in her backpack and walked over to Tony Bates, the town administrator's son.

"I'm gonna check on Mrs. Mitchell. No one I've talked to has seen her since before the hurricane." Without waiting for a response she navigated her way across the minefield of fallen trees and debris toward the old widow's house. She had no idea how old Mrs. Mitchell was, but she guessed she had to be close to eighty. According to her mom, Mrs. Mitchell had been living alone since her daughter moved to North Carolina the previous summer.

The single-story ranch looked exactly as Charlie remembered when she'd taken piano lessons in the fourth grade. White paint covered the exterior while black shutters, several of which were missing, framed each window. The only differences were the shattered glass windows and the fallen trees. An empty hole occupied the spot where the doorbell should have been so Charlie pounded on the front door and waited for a response. When no answer came, Charlie looked through the nearest window but all she saw was an empty living room.

Maybe she went to the basement. Charlie took the steps two at a time. She'd spent enough time at Mrs. Mitchell's house to know that the only way into the basement was through the bulkhead around the side of the house.

When she reached the bulkhead she found a young oak tree lying across it, making it impossible for her to open the door. Getting down on her hands and knees she pounded on the metal door. "Mrs. Mitchell it's Charlotte O'Brien," she shouted. "Are you okay?"

"I can't get the door open," a familiar soft voice answered, sounding frazzled.

Relief washed over her. The elderly woman was safe. "There's a tree covering the door. Are you hurt?"

"I'm hungry and cold, but not hurt."

"Just sit tight and I'll have you out in no time."

Although not huge, the tree would have to be cut up before it could be moved. Cupping her hands around her mouth she called out, "I need some help over here. Bring a chainsaw. Mrs. Mitchell is trapped in the basement."

At the request for help several other volunteers stopped what they were doing and ran over. By the time the others arrived Charlie had already started to pull away some of the loose tree limbs. "Mike, just make the pieces manageable for now. You can cut them smaller later."

Without questioning her orders Mike started the engine on his chainsaw and got to work.

"Kevin, help me with this one," Charlie said as the first section of the tree was sliced off.

It took several trips but eventually Charlie and Kevin moved each section of the tree. Later they would need to be removed from the property but for the time being they were fine lying against the house's foundation.

"Thanks guys." Charlie wiped her damp hands on her pants and walked back to the bulkhead door.

Before gripping the handle, Charlie again knelt down

next to the door. "I'm going to open the door now, Mrs. Mitchell." Wrapping her hand around the cold metal handle, Charlie pulled open the bulkhead door. The groan of rusty hinges assaulted Charlie's ears. Despite its cry of protest the door opened, and Charlie found Mrs. Mitchell huddled on the concrete stairway that led into the basement. The elderly woman looked tired and cold but otherwise fine. Just to be on the safe side, Charlie went down the stairs to offer Mrs. Mitchell help up.

"I didn't think anyone would find me." With a bit of struggle Mrs. Mitchell came to her feet. "I forgot the cell phone my daughter gave me and I couldn't get the door open."

"You had everyone worried. Let me help you up." Charlie held out her hand. "Just to be on the safe side I want to check your vitals."

It wasn't until after Charlie helped Mrs. Mitchell up the last step that she noticed the black Cadillac Escalade parked on the street and the two men standing near it. So the Falmouth Foundation sent its poster boy to the front lines, Charlie thought as she watched Jake Sherbrooke speak with Joseph Bates, Town Administrator. She knew the billionaire playboy was the head of the Falmouth Foundation, a disaster relief organization. The town administrator had mentioned that the foundation was arriving with some much-needed aid. However, she hadn't thought they would send *him*. From what she heard, he didn't strike her as the hands-on type. Rich spoiled men like him acted as the public face of organizations while everyone else did the real work. After all he was not only a member of the Sherbrooke Family, one of the richest families in America, but his father was the President of the United States.

At least he'll be out of here as soon as his photo op is done.

As Jake listened to the town official explain what damage the town suffered, he couldn't keep his eyes off the redhead barking out orders. He figured she could probably make a Marine drill instructor drop and give her fifty push-ups. Normally he didn't go for redheads. He'd always favored brunettes, but he couldn't keep himself from watching her as she helped an elderly woman from her basement. There was an aura of self-confidence emanating from her.

"Like other towns around here we have no electricity and many downed trees. The dam letting go is what really devastated us. All the neighborhoods near the river and lake are flooded. Those between Church Street and Lincoln are in the worst shape. Water levels in some spots have been measured at seven feet," the town administrator explained.

Jake already knew about the dam. In fact that was why he'd chosen North Salem. "What about injuries?" Jake pulled his eyes away from the redhead who was sitting by the older woman, checking her pulse.

"Only three reported casualties. But there are lots of injuries and several people are still unaccounted for. Dr. O'Brien can give you a detailed medical report. She's been handling medical issues in the field."

Jake made a note to check with Dr. O'Brien as soon as he finished with the town official. "How do things stand with shelters?"

"We've already started setting things up at the high school, but it won't be enough. There are not many places ..." Before he could finish his cell phone rang. "If you'll excuse me, I need to take this call," he said after checking the caller ID.

Jake nodded. "No problem." Once the man walked away Jake surveyed the activity around him. It seemed as if everyone around him was active and the few that weren't were simply taking short water breaks. At the head of it all was the redhead. He couldn't help but wonder who she was. She didn't strike him as a town official, yet she gave the appearance of authority and people seemed to listen to her.

Unable to just stand around and do nothing while others worked, Jake figured the redhead was the person to ask where he could help. Ignoring the stares and whispers he got as he walked by, Jake made his way toward the elderly woman's house where the redhead was at work covering up one of the broken windows with some plywood. Stopping close enough so that she would hear him over the pounding hammer without shouting, but far enough away to avoid getting hit by her swings, he was momentarily speechless. From a distance the redhead was pretty, but up close she was downright beautiful. He guessed she was about five-foot seven or so because she stood only a few inches shorter than his six-one. Her fiery red hair was pulled back in a knot and the gray t-shirt and khaki cargo pants she wore did nothing to hide her figure.

"What can I do to help?" Jake asked watching the muscle in her well-defined upper arm flex as she swung the hammer.

"All set here, thanks." The redhead answered without even pausing to look at him.

Despite her cool behavior, Jake wasn't deterred. There was plenty that needed to be done and he sensed that she could direct him to where he could be most useful. "Then point me to where I can help. That's why I'm here," he snapped back, his voice smooth but insistent.

The redhead stopped in mid-swing and turned to look at him, her gaze meeting his eyes. "That other window needs to be covered. I promised Mrs. Mitchell I'd take care of this before I go." The woman nodded toward an open toolbox on the ground. "If you don't want to do that Mary could use some help down at the high school setting up the shelter."

Jake didn't miss the coolness in the woman's voice, but he chose to ignore it. Jake grabbed the hammer from the tool belt around his waist. "Not a problem Ms..."

"Doctor actually, Doctor Charlotte O'Brien."

This was the doctor the town administrator mentioned!

Interesting. With the hammer from his tool belt in one hand, Jake extended the other toward Charlotte. "Jake Sherbrooke."

Charlotte accepted his extended hand. "I know," she said, her mouth spread into a thin-lipped smile. "There is a lot to do. We better get back to work."

She didn't wait for him to answer. Instead she went back to pounding nails and for the most part ignoring him. What is her deal, Jake wondered as he began working. It was obvious that she didn't think much of him. It wasn't a situation he ran into very often. Most people liked him, only occasionally did he come in contact with a wise ass who resented him for who he was – or at least who they thought he was. Thanks to the Sherbrooke name and the media, most of the country thought they knew him. The media liked to portray him as a carefree playboy who never thought of anyone but himself. He let everyone believe it didn't bother him, even his family. But he resented it.

Forget about it. Everyone's under a lot of stress. That's all it is. With thoughts of Doctor O'Brien pushed from his mind, he focused on pounding nails into plywood. He'd done the exact same thing on numerous occasions since starting the Falmouth Foundation, though the media always failed to include that bit in their stories about him. In fact, the media almost never mentioned the foundation when they did a piece on him. And when they did, it was as a side note. That didn't surprise him; the American public preferred to hear about which actress he'd taken to the new movie premier or which model he'd taken to dinner.

Jake pounded the last nail into the wood with more force than necessary at the thought of the media vultures that seemed to shadow his every move. "All done with this one," he said turning to look at the woman next to him. "Anymore?"

Doctor O'Brien put the final nail in the board covering her window then turned to face him before her eyes looked over at the plywood he'd hung. As he watched she ran her gaze over his work and Jake guessed that she expected it to fall at any minute.

"No. All set here. Thanks for the help."

"Where to next?" He saw no reason to stop working now.

For a minute she stood eyeing him, her lips pressed tightly together. "I need to get back to treating injuries but you can take your pick. The Larsons across the street need help or you can check down the street."

Jake looked across the street to where a man wielding a chainsaw worked by himself. It looked like as good a place as any to help. "Across the street it is."

He felt the doctor's eyes on his back as he crossed the front lawn to the edge of the street, but he ignored it. Too much work remained for him to worry about one person's opinion of him.

As Jake approached, a burly man with a long light-brown beard that reminded Jake of a younger version of Santa, killed the engine on his chainsaw.

"Need some help over here?" Jake stopped in front of the dismembered tree trunk.

The other man's eyes narrowed for a moment as he studied Jake and he knew the second the younger version of Santa recognized him. The man's eyes grew wide and his eyebrows shot up.

"Aren't you the President's son?"

"Please call me Jake." Jake extended his free hand. "I'm here with the Falmouth Foundation. What can I help with?"

"Phil Larson," the other man said accepting Jake's hand. "I could use some help covering up this glass slider. Damn tree went right through. If I don't get it covered today my wife won't sleep in the house."

"Let's get to it then."

CHAPTER 2

Charlie took the last bite of the strawberry cereal bar she'd snagged from the pantry and hightailed it out of the kitchen before her mom could rope her into helping cook dinner. The bed and breakfast had no paying guests so her mom and brother had opened its doors to anyone who needed a place to stay. Although they still didn't have electricity back they did have a generator, which meant hot meals and running water.

While she was proud that her family made such a gesture, she had no plans of helping in her mom's well-ordered kitchen. Cooking wasn't one of her skills. If a meal required much more than putting it on a tray in the oven, she was lost. Her mom knew this, so if she did ask for help, Charlie would find herself either washing and chopping vegetables or taking care of the dirty pots and pans. On a normal day she wouldn't mind helping her mom a little in the kitchen, but not today. Every muscle in her body ached and she suspected she could fall asleep standing up. It'd been a long day doing everything from treating injuries to boarding up broken windows. All she wanted to do right now was lay down because she knew tomorrow she'd be doing it all again.

Focused more on what tomorrow might bring, Charlie wasn't paying attention as she rounded the corner into the foyer and ran smack dab into a solid wall of muscle. Large male hands instantly gripped her shoulders to steady her, and the scent of pricey cologne mixed with sweat tickled her nose.

"Sorry about that." Charlie's face burned as she took a step back. Now that she was no longer on top of the solid wall of muscle she'd almost run over, she found herself standing in front of none other than Prince Charming himself, Jake Sherbrooke. Despite what she thought of him and others like him, she had to admit he'd done his fair share of physical labor today, much to her surprise.

"If you're here about a room, we're all filled right now," Charlie said unable to ignore the heat spreading through her body. Even with a sweat-stained face and the large scratch he'd gotten at some point during the day, he still caused her heart rate to accelerate.

Although she didn't think highly of billionaires who'd done nothing to earn their money but be born to the right parents, she couldn't deny that he was devastatingly handsome. No wonder supermodels and actresses dated the guy. He looked even better in person than he did in photos.

Jake released her shoulders and took a step back. "My assistant called earlier and reserved a room for me." His tone remained even and his words were spoken without any hint of an accent.

Did he practice speaking like that? She'd met people from all over the country and everyone regardless of where they came from had some type of accent, but not him. If she didn't know he'd grown up in New England she'd never be able to guess where he'd spent his childhood from his voice alone.

"Mr. Sherbrooke your room is all set," Maureen O'Brien said joining them, her flowered apron still tied around her waist. "We have you in the Hawthorne room. I'll show you up."

Charlie remained silent as her mom and Jake Sherbrooke headed up the stairs. The Hawthorne room had been her bedroom before her mom started taking in boarders to help pay the bills. She'd been twelve when her father walked out and for a full year her mom struggled to keep them afloat. Then a friend suggested Maureen take in some college students from Salem State who didn't have a place on campus. Her mom had continued to do that until a few years ago when she and Sean turned the old Victorian into a bed and breakfast.

Using all the determination she had, Charlie dragged her body up the two flights of stairs to the attic. When the house had originally been built the bedrooms in the attic had been for servants, but since her father left she called the smallest one her bedroom.

The room looked the same as it had the day she left for college. Her mom never changed anything. Dark blue curtains still framed the one window and a light blue bedspread covered the bed. No one used the room. Her mom insisted that it be kept ready for Charlie's visits even though they were few and far between.

Stripping off her dirty clothes, she stepped into the shower in the tiny bathroom that separated her bedroom from what had been her brother's room. For a moment she stood under the stream of lukewarm water. The water in that particular bathroom never got hot but, with only a generator to power everything in the house, it was colder than usual. Despite the temperature the water felt wonderful as it cascaded over her tired body, and she took her time washing away the dirt and sweat.

Warm humid air greeted Charlie a few minutes later as she walked back into her room wrapped in a large faded blue bath towel that had at one time matched the painted walls. Like everything else in the room the towel had been there forever.

Man, were his eyes blue. Charlie caught a glimpse through the window of the Escalade parked outside as she pulled a clean shirt out of the bureau. She'd never seen eyes quite that blue. They reminded her of the sapphires in the heart-shaped pendant her mom owned. The only good piece of jewelry her mom had, it had belonged to Charlie's great-grandmother.

Thinking about Jake Sherbrooke's eyes had her thinking about some of the other attributes she'd noticed about him—the well-muscled chest that her hands had felt when she'd run into him in the foyer and the well-defined biceps she'd seen when he'd been working alongside the rest of the town boarding up windows and clearing debris.

Of course he has a great body; he probably has nothing else to do all day but workout. For a minute Charlie envisioned some of the sailors on the base back in Virginia. Sure some had great physiques but not all. Between their work obligations and families many didn't have the time it required. It's not like he has to work like the rest of us, Charlie thought, pulling her shirt over her head. Unlike her, he'd always had everything at his fingertips: the best clothes, the best cars, the best schools. Though her clothes had been clean they'd always come from consignment stores. She hadn't gotten her own car until after graduating from college, which she'd only been able to afford thanks to the Navy. People like him didn't know what the real world was like.

Charlie started to move away from the window but stopped when she saw movement below. Was she imagining things? After all, she had been standing there thinking about the man and the way he'd looked working today. Taking a step closer to the window she saw her brother and his Irish Wolfhound approaching Jake. After exchanging a few words, the two men started to tackle the large tree limbs covering the front walkway. Despite the fact that he'd already worked for several hours, Jake carried away the limbs once Sean cut them into more manageable pieces with his chainsaw.

Was he always this hands-on? Although there were plenty of other things she could be doing, Charlie stood at the window combing out her wet shoulder-length hair and watching the two men below. Every once in a while the humming of the chainsaw stopped and her brother moved to tackle another enormous limb or said something to their billionaire guest. Although she couldn't hear anything, Charlie guessed her brother was telling their guest some politically incorrect jokes, the only kind Sean knew, because more than once she saw Jake laughing.

"Find something useful to do with yourself." Charlie tossed her hairbrush onto the bureau next to the envelope containing her retirement papers. Picking up the envelope she pulled out the half-completed documents and glanced over them. She'd started to fill them out before leaving Virginia but hadn't finished. At the time uncertainty held her back. She'd hoped some time away from the base and work would help her make a definitive decision. So far it hadn't happened. While she was leaning toward staying with the Navy a tiny part of her wanted to move on with her life.

As if her eyes had a mind of their own, Charlie glanced out the window when she heard her brother's chainsaw stop once again. "You're pathetic." Charlie tossed the documents down and headed toward the bedroom door. Even if her mom put her to work peeling onions it would be a more productive way to spend her time than standing and watching Jake Sherbrooke work. Too bad it wouldn't be as enjoyable.

A little later Charlie was halfway out of the kitchen carrying a platter covered with homemade biscuits, when Sean burst through the kitchen's side door. Jake followed right behind him gripping his left arm.

"Need you over here now, Charlie. Jake's bleeding." Sean's usual confident tone contained a note of concern.

"I told you. It isn't that bad."

For someone injured, Jake didn't sound that concerned to Charlie. Putting the platter down on the counter, she moved toward the kitchen table. "Have a seat and let me take a look. Sean, get me the first aid kit."

Without any argument both men complied. And just like she would with any other patient, Charlie moved closer to get a better look at the bloody open wound which ran from just above his wrist to halfway up his outer forearm. Though the cut was long it didn't appear too deep.

"What happened?" She leaned down for a closer look.

"An old nail and some shards of glass got me when we were trying to get into that old shed."

"When was your last tetanus shot?" Charlie reached for one of the clean wet towels Sean placed on the table along with the first aid kit.

Damn it. If he'd been paying attention to what he'd been doing rather than thinking about the redhead that was now cleaning the area around the wound, he wouldn't be sitting here now. He'd still be outside doing something useful rather than thinking about all the things he'd like to be doing with the good doctor, who didn't look all too happy at the moment.

"Beginning of the year." The barest hint of vanilla teased him every time he inhaled and he knew it wasn't coming from some food in the kitchen. It had to be her shampoo.

Charlie nodded, her short ponytail swinging with the movement. "You can go to the ER if you want but it's not necessary. The cut isn't too deep. I don't think it will even leave a scar, but we'll have to watch for an infection."

There was no way in hell he was going to the ER for a scratch, especially not when the town's residents were already facing some serious injuries. "Just clean and wrap it for me. I'll be fine, Doctor." It'd been on the tip of his tongue to call her Charlotte, but he caught himself at the last second. She'd introduced herself as Doctor Charlotte O'Brien. That told him she didn't want to be on a first-name basis with him, which irked him for some reason although he didn't know why. Maybe because the rest of her family and the people he'd met today had been friendly. Sure he'd gotten a few stares from people but for the most part they'd accepted him into their fold as he worked alongside them. Not true of the good doctor. Her manner had been reserved and aloof from the moment he approached her. He tried to come up with reasons for her attitude, but none came to him.

"You sure he doesn't need stitches?" Sean asked. He remained next to the table as Charlotte worked.

Sean didn't strike him as a worrier by nature. Would Sean be this concerned if he was someone other than Jake Sherbrooke? "I trust the good doctor's judgment. It'll be fine."

Charlie paused in the wrapping of his arm and looked up at him, surprise evident in her beautiful hazel eyes. This close, he could see the tiny flecks of green in them as well as her incredibly long eyelashes. What would her eyes look like glazed over with desire? Would the green flecks be more pronounced? Would the hazel darken?

Focus Jake. You're not here looking for a woman. "It smells delicious in here." Jake hoped to distract himself from the woman in front of him with some small talk.

Reaching for a roll of tape, she tore off a long piece and placed it on his arm. Unable to tear his eyes away, Jake watched her every movement. Her hands were slender with long fingers and short neatly trimmed nails. She wore no rings or nail polish, and with no warning the image of her hands on the rest of his body entered his mind.

"Thanks to our generator we'll all have a hot meal tonight. Ma made enough beef stew to feed a carrier."

Charlie's voice drew him back to the kitchen. Disgusted with himself, he pulled his arm away. Most of the time he had better control than this. Fantasizing about a beautiful woman while sitting in her family's kitchen wasn't something he normally did.

"Sounds good. Thanks for taking care of my arm. I can finish up from here."

Without commenting she handed him the roll of tape and began to clean up the other supplies on the table. She tackled the task just like she seemed to do everything else, efficiently. He wondered if she was like that by nature or because of her Naval training.

"Sean said you're in the Navy. Are you stationed in Virginia?" Jake tore off one last strip of tape and placed the roll back in the first aid kit. "I noticed a car in the parking lot with Virginia plates," he said when she threw him a questioning look.

"Yeah. At least for now."

Jake leaned back in his chair oddly pleased that the cold tone she'd used with him earlier in the day seemed to be thawing out a little. "I'm in Alexandria. Are they planning to transfer you to another base?"

Charlie studied him without saying a word. For a moment it appeared as if she was going to tell him it was none of his business.

"I am thinking about retiring."

"Tough one." Jake hoped he sounded sincere. If he was in her shoes he'd stay in a heartbeat.

She didn't answer but rather shrugged as she washed her hands in the kitchen sink. "Try to keep that clean and dry. I'll check it tomorrow. Supper is being served in the dining room whenever you're ready." With her final statement she dried her hands and disappeared through the swinging door.

Jake stayed seated for several minutes. The picture of her tall lithe body was branded on his mind. She didn't seem to know the kind of effect she had on men. Under different circumstances he would pursue her with no questions asked, but now wasn't the time or place. Not to mention the fact that she seemed to be indifferent to him.

When his stomach growled in protest, Jake stood and pushed his thoughts of Charlotte out of his mind. He hadn't eaten anything other than energy bars since breakfast and the freshly baked biscuits he smelled were calling his name.

***

When Jake's alarm went off the next morning at the crack of dawn, his initial instinct was to hit the snooze button, roll over and go back to sleep. Mornings were not his best time of day, especially this early in the morning, but when he glimpsed the ruffled canopy over his head he remembered where he was and more importantly why he was there.

Grabbing some jeans out of his duffel bag, he pulled them on before searching for a clean t-shirt. Since he'd showered just before hitting the sack the night before, it seemed unnecessary to take another one now. Besides, after the day he expected to have, he knew he would need one later anyway.

Downstairs he followed the voices to the dining room where Maureen O'Brien had set out cereal, muffins and bagels for breakfast. Jake skipped both and zoned in on the coffee where Charlie stood pouring herself a large mug.

"You're up early. I took you as more of a night person," she said sparing him a quick glance.

Jake watched as she poured cream into her coffee. "I'm meeting with the town administrator in about thirty minutes to assess the damage down by the river. And the first shipment of supplies from the foundation is arriving later."

Charlie didn't reply. Rather she studied him over the rim of her coffee mug. "Do you always go where the foundation gives out aid?"

Jake nodded. "There have been a few times that I haven't, but I try to get there."

She made a surprised sound in the back of her throat

but didn't comment.

He didn't know why she was surprised by his answer. She probably knew that he was in charge of the Falmouth Foundation. It wasn't a secret. "You seemed surprised?"

Stepping away from the coffee so someone else could get some, she took a sip before answering. "I assumed you were more of a poster boy for the foundation. I didn't picture you as the hands-on type."

Annoyance swept through his body. She didn't see him as the hands-on type after all the work he'd already done. "And how do you see me?"

Perhaps hearing the anger in his voice, Charlie's eyes narrowed and her back became ramrod straight. "You're not exactly described as the hardest working man alive in the media," she answered matter-of-factly. "According to them you're out with a different woman every night driving around in expensive cars. I assumed someone like that wouldn't be interested in physical labor." Her tone wasn't rude. Rather she sounded as if she was reciting facts from a book.

The media was great at portraying people in a way that was best for their ratings. Very rarely did they get the truth right. This wasn't the first time someone had assumed he was nothing more than a spoiled rich playboy and he was confident it wouldn't be the last. Normally, he would shrug it off. If someone wanted to believe the media's image of him he wouldn't bother with them. However, this time it troubled him. For some reason, he wanted to prove the doctor wrong. He wanted to show her the real Jake Sherbrooke.

"I'm not going to lie. I like fast cars, but a different woman every night isn't my thing. You can't always believe what you read." Jake clenched his teeth to keep his anger from creeping into his voice. "Why don't you spend the day with me? See what I really do." He expected her to say no.

Tilting her head to the side she studied his face. "When

do we leave?"

Jake forced himself not to smile. "Meet me by my truck in ten minutes."

Once again Charlie nodded and then headed in the direction of the kitchen. Jake couldn't help but watch and admire her retreating form. There was no mistaking her confident no-nonsense step. By inviting her along he knew he'd made his day more difficult, but he didn't regret his invitation. Not one bit. Only an insane man would regret having a beautiful woman by his side all day.

After unwrapping the blueberry muffin he'd grabbed before coming outside, he raised it to his mouth. It was still warm from the oven and his mouth watered just looking at it. He bit into it just as his phone rang. With his free hand he pulled the smart phone from his pocket and checked the number.

Blair again. She'd called earlier that week and he thought he'd made it clear that he wasn't interested in getting back together. Part of him wanted to ignore the call and let it go straight to voice mail. If he answered all he'd get was a repeat of their past conversation. If he ignored the call though, she'd only call again. Swallowing his mouthful of muffin, he answered the phone. Better to get the conversation over with now. "I don't have a lot of time Blair. I have an important meeting soon. What's up?"

"I'm heading up to New York City this weekend and I wanted to see if you would join me. I thought maybe some time alone would be good for us."

Jake held back a groan. Time alone would only accomplish one thing; to remind him how ill-suited they were for each other. "I'm in the field right now, Blair. I can't go anywhere."

"Come on. You can sneak away for a weekend. Who'll know? There are others who can do the work."

"Blair, I told you before I'm not interested. We had fun together but it's over." So far he'd tried to be polite about the whole thing but she just didn't get it.

On the other end of the line Blair droned on, but he didn't pay much attention as she reiterated their earlier conversation almost word for word. Instead his gaze focused on Charlie as she approached his SUV with a backpack slung over one shoulder and a travel mug in each hand.

"Listen, I've got to go. I need to head out for my meeting. Have a safe trip to New York." Jake cut Blair off in mid-sentence. He heard Blair mutter goodbye right before he hit the end button and stuffed the phone back into his pocket.

"I thought we might both want some more coffee." Charlie stopped next to him and handed him one of the mugs.

"You read my mind. Only had time for one cup inside." Before she could do it herself, Jake pulled open the passenger door for her.

Surprise skittered across Charlie's face but she only murmured thanks before climbing into the front seat.

"So what's the best way to Church Street?" he asked as he climbed behind the wheel and started the engine.

***

Charlie carried another case of bottled water into the senior center. Situated near the center of town it worked perfectly as a temporary supply distribution center. Outside there were several other volunteers helping to unload the trucks filled with bottled water and canned food, each one sent by the Falmouth Foundation. They had already unpacked one truck containing blankets and clean clothes for those in need.

After dropping the case next to the others she rubbed the dull ache in her back. She'd been working nonstop since climbing into Jake's truck that morning and her body felt it. First they'd met with the town administrator near the flooded areas of town. Together with the fire chief the four of them had gone out by boat so Jake could survey the damage firsthand before heading back to the town official's temporary office in the high school. The high school was one of the few buildings with electricity thanks to the generator supplied by the Falmouth Foundation. Workers were currently delivering the rest of the generators to other key buildings.

After a meeting to discuss what further aid and funds were necessary they headed over to the senior center and converted it into a makeshift distribution center. They finished the job a mere ten minutes before the first supply truck rolled in.

Charlie leaned against the wall. All around her people were coming and going. There wasn't a sole standing still including Jake Sherbrooke himself. When he wasn't carrying supplies off the trucks he was helping people take what they needed to their cars. He treated them all as equals. Never once did he put on any airs and, like the day before, there wasn't any media around taking note like she expected. She was still trying to get her head around that fact. According to what she'd seen yesterday and today, he wasn't at all what she'd expected. And she had to admit, if it wasn't for him and his foundation the town would be in much rougher shape. The governor in Boston had declared a state of emergency for most of the North Shore but few towns had been affected as badly as North Salem. Still, state aid was spread thin and so far they'd received little help from the state itself.

"All the trucks outside are empty. Sherbrooke said the next few won't be here for an hour or so. He wants everyone to take a break." Michael Smith, a former high school classmate, said stopping next to her. "I'm heading home to check on things. "Want a ride?"

At the mention of Jake, she began searching for him. The last she'd seen of him he'd been helping Mr. Wilson carry supplies out to his ancient pickup. "I'm good Michael. I think I'll just stick around here in case someone needs help."

"Suit yourself. See ya later." With his final comment Michael headed towards the main doors with several other volunteers.

In no time the senior center was virtually empty of workers. Only a handful of volunteers remained to distribute items as residents stopped in.

After getting a bottle of water and an energy bar, Charlie pulled a folding chair over to the table and sat down. Damn, it seemed like every time she came home Mother Nature went crazy. The last time she'd come back a blizzard dropped 20 inches of snow on the state. The time before that an early winter nor'easter roared through New England. Maybe Mother Nature was trying to give her a hint. Maybe she should ask her family to visit her instead.

From across the hall, the sound of the main door opening and closing echoed. Looking up just in time, she saw Jake enter the building and she almost sighed like a lovesick teenager. Normally she didn't get all worked up when she saw a good-looking man. She certainly came into contact with enough of them in the military. But there was something about Jake that turned her insides to mush and sent her heart rate into overdrive.

"I thought you might have headed out with everyone else," he said as he crossed the hall toward her.

Jake entered the room and it felt like the temperature jumped twenty degrees. Today he looked more like a hard laborer with his sweat stained Cal Tech t-shirt and torn jeans than a pampered playboy and Charlie's pulse leaped with excitement. She shrugged and reached for another bottle of water. "I thought I would stick around in case anyone showed up looking for something. Besides I'd only have to come back in a little while." Charlie slid the water bottle across the table toward Jake before he could say anything.

Jake downed half the bottle in one long drink. "So what do you think?"

Focused on the perpetual five o'clock shadow Jake seemed to favor, Charlie didn't immediately realize he was talking to her. Typically she didn't like any facial hair on a man. It reminded her too much of her father; he'd always sported a full beard. She could do without any reminders of him. Even after all this time the pain caused by his leaving remained. Yet she didn't mind facial hair on Jake. On him it only added to his sexiness.

"Doctor?"

"Think about what?" What had he asked her?

"You more or less called me a lazy playboy this morning. What do you think now?"

His tone was cool and direct but Charlie thought she detected a hint of vulnerability. Did her opinion matter to him? Could this man, who had everything, be insecure?

"You're not lazy," she answered without any hesitation. Man, she wished she'd chosen her words more carefully this morning. He'd been working just as hard if not harder than everyone else and not because he had to. He didn't live here, didn't have any family here. He could have just as easily directed everything from his office back in Virginia and had an assistant come out to give him updates. "Are you always this involved?"

Jake finished off his water and reached for an energy bar. "Just about. The foundation is my baby. I like to make sure it's being run properly. I can't do that by sitting behind a desk all day."

If what she had seen here was any indication, the foundation and its employees ran like a well-oiled machine. Whatever else Jake Sherbrooke might be, he was a good leader. "I'm glad you offered aid. The town hasn't gotten a lot of support so far from the state."

Jake rolled his shoulders as if trying to work out some stiffness and Charlie couldn't help but notice the way his chest muscles rippled under his shirt. Without warning, memories of how that chest felt under her hands when she'd crashed into him the day before filled her mind. The memory brought an instant twinge of desire to her insides, and she found herself wondering what it would be like to be held against his broad chest.

"The states have limited resources. They do the best they can but there's too much bureaucracy. That's one of the reasons I started the relief foundation."

His words cut through her momentary day dream. "You started it?" She could hear the utter disbelief in her voice and the expression on Jake's face told her he had heard it as well.

"Even we playboys need something to do during the day when we are not cruising around in our expensive cars looking to pick up women." Jake's voice was both sarcastic and amused at the same time.

Nice going. You've managed to insult him twice in one day. "I'm sorry. Really I didn't mean to..."

"You need to stop listening to the media, Doc. More than half of what they print is either pure BS or skewed beyond belief."

Charlie opened her mouth to reply but the cell phone in Jake's pocket went off at that exact moment.

"I need to take this. It's my assistant in Virginia."

Without another word he left, leaving Charlie to wonder what else the media got wrong about Jake.

For the rest of the afternoon Charlie didn't see much of Jake. He had not spoken to her again after his phone call. Whether or not that was because he was annoyed by her earlier comments, she didn't know. After hanging up with his assistant he spent some time making other calls before the last few supply trucks rolled in and the volunteers returned to unload them. Every once in a while Charlie got the feeling that someone was watching her, but only once did she catch Jake eyeing her.

He's probably right, she thought as she helped carry things out to Mrs. Anderson's car. The news and media rarely got the important news right, so why would it get anything else right? Besides she should know by now not to judge a person without getting to know them. And even if Jake was a rich playboy who went from woman to woman it didn't matter right now. All that mattered was that the town got the help it needed.

Turning to head back inside, Charlie stopped when she saw a short chubby figure running up the road toward the senior center. At first the person was too far away to make out a face, but when the individual got closer Charlie recognized the runner. Jessica Quinn lived at the bottom on the hill with her grandparents.

Panting, Jessica all but collapsed at Charlie's feet when she reached her. "My grandfather...fell...off... the ladder. Can't … get...up. No...phone or ...car."

Charlie didn't wait for Jessica to continue. She knew Jessica's grandfather and a fall from a ladder could kill a man his age. "Don't move."

Without any hesitation Charlie bolted into the senior center. Thankfully Jake stood just inside when she entered. "I need a ride *now*."

Jake pulled his keys from his pocket. "Let's go." He didn't need any further explanation. He knew by her expression it must be important. Before he could say anymore, she rushed back out the door and was half way to his SUV.

"Where to?"

"Down the hill to the big old yellow house. Jessica's grandfather fell." Charlie nodded towards the other woman who climbed into the backseat of the SUV. Charlie handed the woman her cell phone. "It's 911, tell them what happened."

Gravel and dust kicked up as Jake sped out of the parking lot and he listened as Jessica answered the 911 dispatcher's questions from the backseat.

"He turned eighty last month. He wasn't moving when I left. Please hurry." Jessica's voice quivered and he sped up. He could only imagine how she must be feeling.

There was no missing the huge monstrosity of a house with the crooked wooden sign hanging out front that read Blackthorne Farm; it was the only house on that stretch of road.

Before the truck came to a full stop Charlie opened the door and jumped out. Throwing the truck into park, Jake watched as she sprinted across the lawn toward the prone figure on the ground. Would it be better if he kept Jessica back at the truck, out of the way? An upset granddaughter might make the situation worse. Then again, Charlie might need help and who knew how long it might take for the EMTs to arrive. He'd passed the fire station on his way into town so he knew it was located on the other side of town.

Pulling the keys out of the ignition, Jake looked back at Jessica whose breathing remained labored from her run. "You're welcome to stay and wait here. I'm going to see if the doctor needs help."

Jessica shook her head causing her light brown bangs to fall into her eyes. "I want to be with him and my grandmother."

Jake could see the worry and fear etched on her tear-stained face. He could understand her desire to be with her family. After getting out himself, he pulled open her door and helped her out of the SUV. Then he grabbed the first aid kit from the trunk and he followed Jessica up to the house where a seven-foot ladder remained propped against the house. On the ground lay an unmoving figure, his white hair covered in blood and his left arm bent at an unnatural angle. Next to him sat a weeping woman with a long gray braid and glasses.

"He's breathing but unconscious. His pulse is strong though," Charlie said when they joined her. "I need something for his head. He's got a nasty gash and is losing more blood than I'm comfortable with. There is no question that his left arm is broken."

Jake handed her the gauze pads from the kit, impressed

at how calm and collected she remained as she continued to do an assessment of the elderly man. She didn't appear fazed at all by the situation unlike the two crying women kneeling next to the man.

"His neck looks fine, but I don't want to move him. His skin feels cool. Is there an emergency blanket in the kit?"

A quick search turned up the blanket the doctor wanted. Jake tore open the package and covered the injured man with the metallic-colored blanket. "What else can I do?" He felt useless standing there as she worked.

Charlie didn't say anything, she only nodded toward Jessica who had started to sob uncontrollably the minute she saw the blood.

Nodding to let Charlie know he understood, he leaned down and placed a gentle hand on Jessica's shoulder. "We should move so we're not in the way." Jake tugged Jessica and her grandmother to their feet and led them past the driveway where a Honda Accord sat squashed beneath a huge tree and towards the farmer's porch.

"I've never seen a car that flat before. Have you?" It was a stupid statement but his intent wasn't to have an intelligent conversation. He meant to distract the women. In the distance the wail of an ambulance siren could be heard and he feared its arrival would only distress them even more. "I think you might need a new car."

Jake managed to get Jessica and her grandmother into rocking chairs on the farmer's porch. His ridiculous statement about the car earned him half a smile. "That tree had some nerve falling on the car like that." The sound of tires going over rocks told him the ambulance had arrived.

Jake kept up as steady stream of chatter and used his body to block Jessica's view of her grandfather as the EMTs secured him to a stretcher. It appeared as if he still had not regained consciousness, and, by the way the responders had moved him from the ground to the stretcher, he assumed they were worried about possible neck and back injuries too. In a young person either of those injuries could be difficult to heal from, but in a person his age they could be life altering.

"I'm riding to the hospital with them," Charlie called over as they wheeled the stretcher toward the ambulance.

Jake almost suggested that Jessica or her grandmother ride in the ambulance instead, but changed his mind at the last minute. The women weren't exactly calm and they might get in the way. Besides, an extra set of experienced hands might be useful on the way to the hospital. "We'll meet you there." If the tables were reversed he'd want to be at the hospital and the pancake of a car in the driveway wasn't going anywhere.

Charlie threw him a thumbs-up and pulled the ambulance doors closed behind her.

***

Jake grabbed the box of tissues from a table in the hospital waiting room and brought it over to Jessica and her grandmother. They had been there for almost two hours and already the two women had gone through five of the tiny boxes of tissues the hospital left out for patients.

"Here are some more." Jake handed Jessica the box and then took the seat next to her again. Like everything else in the room it was cheap but functional. "Can I get you anything? Some water?" His eyes darted across the room to the vending machines in the corner. The row of colorful machines provided the only color in the stark white room. "A snack?"

Jessica pulled out a few tissues before handing the box to her grandmother. "No, thanks. I'm fine," she said between sniffles. "This is my fault. I should have gone up the ladder." Her voice cracked as she spoke. "Or made him wait till someone else could come by."

The anguish and guilt he heard in Jessica's voice had him putting his arm around her shoulder. "It wasn't anyone's fault. It just happened." What else could he say?

"He's right Jess. Your grandpa wouldn't have listened anyway. You know how stubborn he is." It was the first time Mrs. Quinn had spoken since they'd left the house.

"I just wish we knew something. What is taking so long?"

"Dr. O'Brien is with him. As soon as she knows something, she'll tell you." As if by magic the minute he spoke her name, Charlie walked through a door marked "Hospital Employees Only". When she saw the three of them sitting together she paused briefly before continuing toward them. From her expression he couldn't determine what kind of update she was about to deliver. Unlike the women sitting next to him, Charlie seemed remarkably able to control her emotions. Perhaps one had to in order to be a doctor. He had never thought about it before.

"You can come and see him now. It might still be awhile before he is moved to his own room, but you can both sit with him until then."

Neither Jessica nor her grandmother waited to hear another word. Both came to their feet and started toward the door leading back to the patient examining rooms. He expected Charlie to follow right behind them, but she didn't.

"Thank you for bringing them over."

He could see the surprise in her hazel eyes but didn't understand it. Had she thought he would leave the two women back at their house with no way to get here? He had told her he would meet her here. Or was she surprised to find him still in the waiting room with the Quinns? While sitting in a hospital emergency room was rather low on his list of fun things to do, he couldn't in good conscience just drop them off and leave.

"Not a problem."

CHAPTER 3

It had been four days since Charlie walked into the emergency waiting room to get Jessica Quinn and her grandmother and found Jake with his arm around Jessica's shoulder in an attempt to comfort her. She'd expected Jake to drop Jessica and her grandmother off and then leave. She'd been even more surprised to find him still sitting there an hour later when she'd been ready to leave.

That afternoon she started to re-assess her opinion of him. From everything she'd seen he was nothing like the man they portrayed in the media. He came across as a caring and compassionate person who wasn't afraid to get his hands dirty, someone she could easily see herself dating if he lived in town. But he didn't. After this crisis passed he would move on to another one and probably forget about this little town. Not that she would blame him. North Salem wasn't the most interesting place in the world, especially compared to the places he could travel to whenever he got the urge.

You haven't exactly lived in a bubble. Charlie poured cream into her coffee and then mixed in sugar. Thanks to the Navy she'd been to parts of the world she never would've seen otherwise. While many of the places weren't vacation hot spots, she'd still gotten away from Massachusetts, unlike her mother and brother. Both of them had spent their whole lives on the East Coast. Had her mom been any further south than Virginia? She'd never stopped to think about it before now, but she didn't think so.

What places had Jake been to? She'd just started to make a mental list of all the places their billionaire guest had probably been when he walked into the dining room.

"Good morning. Please tell me there is more coffee."

Charlie didn't bother to stifle her laugh. It seemed as if she and Jake had at least one thing in common. They were both addicted to coffee. "You're as bad as me. Ma just made some more." She pointed to the coffee urn on the sideboard. "She made some muffins too."

She knew it was rude to stare, but that didn't stop her from following Jake with her eyes as he walked across the room. His dark blond hair was still damp from his shower and tiny droplets of water trickled down his neck. Her fingers itched to walk up behind him and wipe the water away. Balling her hands into tight fists, Charlie waited for the irrational thought to disappear.

After he poured himself some coffee and picked out a muffin Jake took the seat across from her. "I'm glad you're here. After I meet with the engineers working on the dam problem, I'm heading over to visit Mr. Quinn. I thought you might like to join me."

As feared Mr. Quinn broke both his hip and left arm in the fall. On the bright side however, he hadn't done any damage to his back or neck.

"When I stopped in to see him yesterday he asked about you, Doc."

Charlie knew Jake had stopped in to see Mr. Quinn every day since the accident. Jessica had told her when she called the day before. But she hadn't visited him yet herself.

"I'll be down at the high school. Pick me up before you head over." She'd volunteered to help keep an eye on the town's children so that their parents could start salvaging what they could from their homes and take stock of the damage, two tasks that would be nearly impossible with children in tow.

Jake stood and grabbed another muffin from the basket. "Your mom should open her own bakery. Her baking is incredible."

"I've told her that, but she doesn't believe me. Maybe you should tell her."

"Next time I see her I will." Jake put his empty coffee cup down on the table. "I'm heading out now, but I will see you this afternoon probably sometime after lunch." Without waiting for a response, he disappeared out the door.

Charlie sat staring at the door long after it closed. Images of him standing there in his well-worn jeans and dark blue polo shirt filled her mind. No matter what the guy wore he seemed to look incredible. He was the kind of person who could throw on a potato sack and still look ridiculously sexy. Without intending to she started to imagine just what he looked like without his clothes on. His shoulders were broad and his arms well-defined and tanned. Though she didn't have any proof, she envisioned him with powerful pecs and a sculpted six-pack. Propping her head up against her hand she mentally sighed at the vision in her head.

"Thought you were heading over to the school for nine?" Her mom's voice cut through Charlie's daydream and her vision of Jake naked evaporated. "What?" she asked whipping her head around.

"A little distracted this morning? Everything okay?" Concern laced her mother's voice.

"Just zoned out for a minute. I have a lot on my mind. Yeah, I am going to the high school. I want to grab some coffee first."

Her mom pointed to the freshly baked muffins. "Take one with you. Who knows when you'll get lunch."

Charlie didn't argue. Her mom was right and besides her mom's banana nut muffins were to die for. The only person who made muffins nearly as good was her friend and roommate Beth. Jake hadn't lied. Her mom should open her own bakery. "I'll see you later." Charlie started towards the door, but then stopped. "Call me if you need anything."

"Don't worry. Your brother is here."

The comment was innocent enough but it still felt like a tiny knife to her heart. Her mom never needed her. As long as she had Sean around, her mom was fine. How different things might have been if her father hadn't walked out on them and forced Sean to become the man of the house. Would this invisible gap exist between them? There was no way to know for certain but Charlie didn't think so. After all it had only developed after her father left and her mom started to depend more and more on Sean.

"Love you, Ma." The words flew out of her mouth before her brain realized it. She didn't say it often but it was true.

"I know. I love you too Charlie." Maureen put down the dirty dishes she held and wrapped her arms around her daughter. "I'm glad you're home."

***

Jake entered the high school just before one o'clock. The meeting with his engineers had gone well. The river's water level was receding; and the engineers had completed their assessment and were developing a plan for rebuilding the dam. The head of the highway department had also called him to set up a meeting about repairing the parts of the roads that had buckled from the onslaught of water.

Yet his good mood wasn't purely due to the progress that was being made. A big part of it was due to the unusual sense of anticipation that coursed through his body. It'd been with him since his run-in with the good doctor that morning. Most people, especially women, jumped at the chance to be with him in the hopes of gaining some of his fame or fortune. Doctor Charlotte O'Brien was not one of these women. She was making him work for her respect. While she'd thawed toward him, she hadn't tried to get to know him. And for reasons that were not entirely clear to him, he wanted to get to know her better. True friends were hard to come by and he got the impression that with some work she could be one.

Or maybe something more, his body suggested when he walked into the school's auditorium. About ten children of various ages were running around playing an indoor version of tag while another ten or so were listening to a story on the stage. Charlie sat in the middle, dressed in a pair of loose-fitting well-worn jeans and a tank top. Typically he didn't find anything attractive about the tomboy look. He'd always preferred a more sophisticated look on women. Yet on the good doctor it looked natural and he found it to be a real turn-on.

When no one noticed his entrance, Jake leaned against the wall and watched Charlie as she interacted with the children gathered around her. Her voice was strong and confident as she read from the picture book she held. The children around her hung on her every word, captivated as much by the story as by her voice. Jake found himself content to just stand there and listen.

It wasn't until she read the last page and closed the book that she noticed him. A small tentative smile spread across her face as she waved in his direction and immediately Jake felt his body respond.

What the hell? She smiled at you. She didn't get naked. Jake mentally shook his head in amazement. Since when did a simple smile turn him on? Maybe it was true what they said about there being a first time for everything.

"All set to go, Doc?" Jake kept his gaze focused on Charlie, determined to ignore the glances the other two women in the room were throwing his way.

Charlie nodded as she stood. "Just let me tell Lizzie I'm going."

Jake couldn't tear his eyes away from Charlie's long legs eating up the stage as she crossed it and headed down the stairs. After a few words with a petite woman with jet black hair who he guessed was Lizzie, she joined him.

She leaned close to him and her arm brushed against his. "I owe you one for rescuing me," she said, her voice a whisper.

Unable to stop himself he laughed at the sincerity in her voice. "Daycare not your thing, Doc?" He pushed open an auditorium door that led into the parking lot.

"Call me Charlie. Everyone does. No it's not my thing. One or two at a time is fine but that was worse than Officer Development School."

He'd been calling her Doc for the past four days. Not once during that time had she corrected him till today, and damn if he wasn't pleased because of it. After opening the passenger door, he waited for her to climb in. "You looked pretty comfortable up there. The kids couldn't take their eyes off you."

Not that I blame them. He closed the door and walked around to the driver's side of the SUV.

Taking a water bottle out of her backpack, she took a drink before answering. "I read four or five books today. Before that we did arts and crafts. Even when I was a kid, I hated that stuff."

Jake smiled at the exasperation in her voice. "Guess it's a good thing you didn't go into teaching like my sister Callie. She spends every day surrounded by twenty or so kids. Honestly, I don't know how she does it, but she insists that she loves it."

"She's the one marrying Dylan Talbot, right?"

He didn't know if she was asking to make polite conversation or because she really didn't know which sister he was talking about. Jake didn't think that was possible, not after last year when everyone including Callie learned that Warren Sherbrooke was her father.

"Yes. Their wedding is in a couple weeks."

Charlie looked as if she was putting together the pieces of a puzzle in her head. "And Dylan's your half-brother?"

Jake nodded prepared to give the explanation to yet another person. "Dylan and I have the same mom, but different fathers. Callie and I have the same dad and different mothers so, yes, I am related to both of them but Callie and Dylan are not related." He couldn't understand why people found the whole thing so confusing.

"You have to admit it's a little odd. It's not something that happens every day."

He agreed with her on that point. Still it wasn't that difficult to understand.

"She's not still teaching though, is she?"

He noticed how the tone of Charlie's voice changed from inquiry to amazement.

Pulling into a parking space in the hospital lot, Jake turned off the ignition. "Why wouldn't she be? She's been doing it since college."

Charlie's eyebrows shot up. "Her father is the President of the United States, and her soon-to-be-husband is a billionaire. It's not like she has to. She could spend her day doing anything she wants."

It wasn't the first time the news that his half-sister continued to teach shocked someone, and he knew that Charlie wouldn't be the last.

Jake got out of the truck and walked around so he could open her door, but he wasn't quick enough. So instead he held out a hand to help her down. Surprise crossed her face again, but she accepted his hand and stepped down.

"Would you stop being a doctor if you didn't have to work?" he asked without releasing her hand. While he waited for her answer his eyes zeroed in on her pale pink lips. His mind suddenly wouldn't let him think about anything but how they would feel against his. As if drawn by an invisible cord he took a step closer.

Charlie ran her tongue over her lips and Jake followed

its path with his eyes, his desire to kiss her growing like a wild fire out of control.

"No, of course not. I guess I can't imagine enjoying being surrounded by that many children every day," she answered, her voice not sounding as confident as usual to him.

Without stopping to think, Jake began to lower his head toward her. "I agree with you there," he whispered inches from her lips.

Charlie didn't stop to think about what was happening or where she was as she felt Jake's lips come down on hers. One of his hands still held hers while the other settled on the curve of her shoulder. The skin on his hand was rough and callused, more proof that he was more than just the face of the foundation. His lips were firm as he slowly kissed her. Unable to stop herself, Charlie took a step closer eliminating the space between them. Then she wrapped her free arm around his lean waist. The additional contact of their bodies seemed to throw a switch in both of them. Jake moved them backward until Charlie leaned back against the SUV. At the same time she teased his lips open with her tongue. Freeing her hand from his, she buried her fingers in his short thick blond hair. Incredible warmth raced through her body as the kiss continued and everything but the man next to her faded from reality.

Only when Charlie heard the sirens of an approaching ambulance did the haze of desire start to clear from her brain and she pulled away. Oh, god! They were in a parking lot making out like a couple of teenagers, in front of a hospital of all places.

Though they stopped kissing, Jake's hand remained on her shoulder and Charlie found herself trapped between wanting to run from him as fast as she could and wanting to pull his head back down toward hers for another kiss.

"We should go inside." She didn't recognize her own

breathless voice as she let her hands fall back to her sides.

Jake trailed a finger down her cheek. "Yeah," he drawled, not moving away.

Charlie's eyes fluttered closed at his gentle caress and in a heartbeat she knew that if she wasn't careful she could fall for this man in a way she'd never fallen before. When it came to the opposite sex she picked only those men she knew she wouldn't get emotionally attached to. There was no way she was going to let a man hurt her the way her dad had hurt her mom when he walked out. To this day she could remember how depressed and withdrawn her mom had become after her dad left. It'd been as if her mom had been replaced by a different person. Her mom hadn't been the only one to change. Sean matured virtually overnight, going from regular high school football player to the man of the house. She'd changed too.

For months after her dad left she'd cried herself to sleep. Once that phase passed she'd started to shield herself emotionally by making sure she didn't let anyone get too close; especially those of the opposite sex. She no longer thought about doing it. It just came naturally. Yet, despite years of emotionally distancing herself from people, somehow Charlie knew if she wasn't careful she could fall for this man. Under no circumstance could she let that happen. So although it went against her body's desires, she moved enough to the right so that she was no longer trapped between Jake's SUV and his muscular body.

"Come on. Mr. Quinn is waiting for you." This time Charlie didn't wait for a response. She started toward the hospital entrance. She heard him fall into step next to her, but refused to look over at him as they entered the hospital's main lobby. She remained silent, keeping as much space between them as possible without seeming obvious, while they waited for the elevator.

When the elevator doors opened, he allowed her to enter before him and she realized for the first time what a gentleman he was. It hadn't struck her until then how rare it was that he always opened doors for her or allowed her to precede him into a room.

Hitting the button for the fifth floor, he turned to her. "Mr. Quinn will be happy you're here. Yesterday he couldn't stop talking about you."

Charlie breathed a sigh of relief at Jake's choice of conversation. While waiting for the elevator she feared he'd say something about their parking lot make out session. Something she didn't want to discuss now or ever. However, a conversation about Mr. Quinn she could handle.

"Jessica and I were friends in school. I spent a lot of time at their house growing up."

Jake's eyebrows came together in confusion.

"What?" she asked.

At first he just shrugged as the elevator doors opened on the fifth floor. "After you." He gestured toward the door.

Bothered by the look of confusion on his face, she couldn't let the matter go. "What was that look for?" she asked inhaling the familiar scent of the hospital. Most people found the smell unsettling but not her. It comforted her.

"She doesn't seem anything like you. I just don't see you two as friends."

Not about to go into great detail, Charlie kept her answer short. "We're more alike than you think. We used to have a lot of the same interests when we were younger, and her parents divorced when she was young too." She didn't give him a chance to question her any further. Instead she pushed open the door to room 506.

Jessica and Martha Quinn sat inside the hospital room with Mr. Quinn and when Charlie walked in all three of their faces lit up. Jake knew inviting her along had been a good idea. After a short conversation about the man's health the three of them began catching up.

"Do you remember the Lindsey twins from high school – the ones we went on that double date with?" Jessica asked, her voice not much louder than a whisper.

Jake thought it fit Jessica perfectly. It was a voice you could easily miss and overlook, much like Jessica herself. That had been one reason he found it odd that she and Charlie were friends. Charlie wasn't the type you could ever overlook.

"How could I forget them?" Charlie rolled her eyes and Jake guessed their double date had been less than ideal.

"Zack was in town last month. You'd never recognize him. He looks like the Pillsbury Dough Boy these days." A deep contagious laugh escaped from Charlie and Jake instantly smiled at the sound. Content to just sit and listen as the two women reminisced about the double date they'd once shared, Jake leaned back in the stiff plastic chair and watched. Away from recovery work and surrounded by friends, Charlie underwent a total transformation. The commanding take-charge air that seemed an integral part of who she was dulled, and her very kissable lips were curved in a permanent smile.

Damn, her lips had felt perfect against his. And right now as he sat here, their kiss dominated his thoughts. When he woke up this morning making out with Charlie in the hospital parking lot had not been on his to-do list. Yet when she stepped down from his SUV, he hadn't been able to stop himself. Despite what the tabloids said about him, he wasn't really a playboy. Yeah, he dated and had been in several relationships but it wasn't like he slept with every other woman in America like the media made it seem. Yet when she touched his hand an invisible cord had pulled him towards her. Nothing could have stopped him from kissing her at that moment.

"How'd your meeting go?" Mr. Quinn asked, his surprisingly gruff voice interrupting Jake's thoughts. "Those engineers of yours making any progress?"

For the next several minutes, Jake explained the ongoing plans to rebuild the town. His surprise that the older man understood even the most technical terms must have shown on his face.

"I studied to be an engineer before the war broke out. Decided to drop out and join the Marines, and then got shipped off to Korea."

He couldn't help but respect the guy. Mr. Quinn had put his country and fellow man ahead of himself. How much easier it would've been for him to stay in school and finish his degree.

"My parents were mighty disappointed too. They tried to talk me outta it but I wouldn't budge. I was a stubborn SOB back then. Some would say I still am." Mr. Quinn looked over at his wife.

Jake could relate to that. His parents had done the same thing when he'd shared his plans to apply to the Naval Academy while still in prep school. Unlike Mr. Quinn though, he'd let their opinion influence his decision.

Thinking about how he'd failed to follow his dreams because of his parents' wishes always put him in a foul mood. Today was no different. Deciding that a few minutes alone would be good, Jake stood. "I'm going to grab some coffee downstairs. Anyone want anything?" After jotting down how everyone wanted their coffee, Jake retreated from the room.

Neither Jake nor Charlie said a word on the ride back to the Victorian Rose a few hours later. Though his mood had improved, the sense of failure that always plagued him whenever he thought about his past weighed heavily on him. If he could only go back in time and redo things.

"You seemed to hit it off with Mr. Quinn." Charlie broke the silence in the SUV as they pulled onto her street. It had been reduced to one lane as repair trucks worked to restore electricity, and he had to wait for his turn. "He doesn't usually take to outsiders."

Jake navigated his way around a utility truck. "Must be

my charming personality. I knew it worked well on the ladies, but it must work well on retired Marines as well."

"Must be it," she agreed laughing.

Despite his best effort Jake couldn't maintain his serious expression at the sound of her laughter.

"Maybe you should consider going into politics. With that charm of yours who knows how far you'd go. You could end up in the White House, too."

He knew Charlie only meant to tease him, yet her words struck a sour chord in him. Politics held no interest for him despite his parents' best efforts. Although it was a big part of his family history, he had no intention of following that path.

The smile that had tugged at his mouth died. "I'll stick with what I'm doing." Jake stopped the Escalade next to Charlie's Jeep in the parking lot. "Washington doesn't interest me. Too much BS." Jake opened his door before she could respond hoping she'd take the hint. It didn't work though.

"Really?" Charlie stepped down after he pulled open her door. "I figured your family had a gene for politics."

Her tone remained light and jovial but he knew she was only half joking. Everyone in America knew that the Sherbrookes had been involved in politics for years.

Jake crossed his arms across his chest. "That gene must have skipped me. Maybe my sister Sara got it."

"Speaking of politics I thought every member of the President's family got Secret Service protection. Where's yours?"

In the five months since he told the Secret Service to take a hike, no one had commented on their absence. Obviously, Charlie was more astute than most. "I refused their protection about two weeks after my father took office. I couldn't stand having them around."

"You can do that?" Charlie's voice echoed the surprise on her face.

Jake let his arms relax and hang by his sides. "Nobody

has before, but yeah." He didn't intend to say anything else on the matter.

***

The battery powered alarm clock on her nightstand read midnight but Charlie stared at the ceiling wide awake. Her body cried out for sleep but her brain hadn't gotten the message yet. It knew Jake slept one floor below, and snapshots of their kiss kept playing through her mind. The feel of his lips on hers and his hand on her skin were forever burned into her memory. Yet that alone wasn't what kept her awake. The pull she felt toward him was what kept her up. She didn't need or want a man in her life. Letting someone in like that only made you vulnerable. Just look what it had done to her mom. No matter what she wasn't going to end up like that, and she knew she'd find herself in the exact same spot if she wasn't careful around Jake. Granted some of her first impressions of him seemed wrong, but that didn't mean he wasn't a heart breaker, especially considering the different worlds they lived in. Though he seemed like a nice guy, he didn't know what it was like to work for what you wanted. He'd always had everything handed to him. She doubted there was single thing in his life he'd ever wanted to do that he had not been able to do.

How much longer will he be here anyway? A few days? Maybe a week tops? I can handle that. Fed up with tossing and turning in bed, Charlie tossed off the covers and headed downstairs for a snack. At this time of night everyone would be in bed so she didn't bother with a robe, besides it wasn't like her boxer shorts and tank top didn't cover everything.

A battery-powered lantern on the kitchen table provided the only light in the room. Though the generator gave the house power, they'd limited its use to the appliances to conserve gas. If they ran out of gas and the generators died, they'd lose her mom's cooking, something no one wanted to do without.

Charlie finished making a sandwich and was about to cover the peanut butter jar when she heard someone enter the kitchen.

"I'm not the only one up." Jake's voice sent a tingle down her spine. Dressed in a white sleeveless t-shirt and sweatpants, he looked devilishly handsome.

At first she stood there staring at him, her mouth dry and her pulse quickening. Finally after what seemed like an eternity she pulled her eyes away from him. "Just making a snack. Want one?"

"I'll never turn down food."

She could feel his eyes on her as she started making another sandwich. Though she didn't usually think much about her appearance and what men thought of her, she couldn't help wonder how Jake saw her. If his kiss was anything to go by, he liked what he saw. "Strawberry or grape jam?" she asked holding up the jars.

"Surprise me," he answered dropping into a spindle-backed chair.

Charlie spread a thin layer of her mom's homemade strawberry jam on Jake's sandwich then added a handful of chips to both plates before carrying them over to the table. "Enjoy." She placed one plate in front of Jake before sitting in the chair next to him.

For several minutes they ate in silence, but she sensed every move he made. Her body seemed to be on high alert just waiting for the moment when his arm would brush against hers or his knee would bump against her leg.

"Couldn't sleep?" Charlie asked, looking for a way to distract herself from the fact she wanted to pull the sandwich from his hands and kiss him.

Jake shook his head no. "Too much on my mind."

Had he been lying in bed thinking about their kiss too? Did he want to repeat it as much as she did or had he already forgotten about it? Did recovery issues occupy his thoughts instead?

"Same here," she said even though he hadn't asked why

she was up.

Pushing back her chair, she was about to ask him if he wanted anything to drink when he reached for her hand. The slight touch sent her heart racing and she swallowed down the nervous laugh she felt rising in her throat.

"About this afternoon," Jake said interlacing their fingers.

The simple action had Charlie's insides quivering. *Please don't apologize.* She'd be mortified if he did that.

Jake didn't say anything else however. Instead his gaze traveled over her face and searched her eyes for a few heartbeats before leaning toward her and picking up right where they'd left off at the hospital.

The feel of his lips against hers was even better than the memory and at his gentle prodding she parted her lips to give him entry. As their tongues met, she wrapped her arms around his neck letting herself get swept away by the unfamiliar emotions his simple kiss awakened.

Gently she felt him work her hair free of its bun and his hands dug themselves into her hair anchoring her to him as he teased her tongue with his. Then without warning she felt his hands drop to her waist and she willingly went when he tugged her onto his lap.

Charlie allowed herself to fall under the spell of his kiss for a few seconds before pulling back. The minute her lips left Jake's she regretted her decision though. Yet she didn't try to kiss him again. Instead she analyzed and waited. The smoldering flame she saw in his eyes told her Jake was affected just as much by their kiss as she was. Briefly, she wondered if she mirrored his look.

"What are your plans for tomorrow?" Jake traced a finger up and down her arm leaving a trail of goose bumps on her bare skin.

"Not sure. I thought I'd see who needed help in the morning."

As he let his hand roam over her shoulder, he seemed to focus on the pulse in her neck and Charlie wondered if he could see how rapid it beat.

"I'm driving to Boston to meet with the Governor for lunch. Come with me. Afterward we can get dinner."

Was he asking her on a date? It sounded like it. She hadn't been on a date in months and it would provide a nice break from the work she'd been doing since the storm.

"Won't Governor Wentworth mind? If he wants to meet with you, it must be important."

Jake shrugged and she couldn't help but notice how broad his shoulders were under her hands.

"He said he wanted to thank me for all the aid the foundation has provided. Honestly I think he's hoping a little ass kissing will help his cause. He wants my father's support in the upcoming election," he explained with a bored tone. "So I really don't care if he minds or not."

"When?" she asked stalling to give herself more time. Normally she didn't have a problem making decisions. It was a trait that came in handy as a doctor. Yet sitting on his lap in the darkened kitchen with his hands on her bare skin, she wavered back and forth.

"I'm meeting him around noon."

It's a couple of meals, no big deal. Charlie tried to ignore his gentle caress up and down her arm. "OK."

A slow sensual smile spread across Jake's face causing red hot desire to shoot through her body. Right then she wanted nothing more than to invite him back up to her room to see what Prince Charming looked like without his clothes on. She had an excellent imagination, but there was no substitute for the real thing.

Bad idea, Charlie. Very bad idea. Though it took every ounce of will power she possessed, Charlie slid off Jake's lap and cleared the empty plates off the table. She needed something to do otherwise she risked jumping back into his arms.

She put the paper dishes in the trash and turned back toward him. "I think I'll head back up now. I'm finally tired."

What looked to be disappointment swept across Jake's face but he didn't try to stop her as she headed toward the swinging kitchen door. "See you in the morning, Charlie."

CHAPTER 4

Jake rubbed the back of his neck and wished he had a couple Motrin on hand as he exited the Governor's mansion the following afternoon. As he'd expected Governor Wentworth had asked him to meet more because he wanted his father's support than because he appreciated the foundation's aid. The Governor would be running for a second term in the next election and figured the backing of a popular President would help his cause. The entire two hours had been miserable. In fact it would've been unbearable if not for Charlie's company. She kept rather quiet during the conversation. Actually, he got the impression that politics wasn't her thing either, but the little she did contribute was insightful. And just her presence there lifted his spirits because he knew once they left he had her all to himself for the rest of the day.

Opening the passenger door for Charlie, he briefly wondered if they should head back to town. Plenty of recovery work still needed to be done. Was it fair of them to skip town for the afternoon? Part of him said no. The more people working, the faster the town would return to normal. The devil in him said the town would survive without them for a few hours. It wasn't like they were skipping town for a week. Besides who knew how much longer he'd be in North Salem. He might not get another chance like this one.

By the time Jake walked around to the driver's door and climbed in his SUV, his mind was made up. Despite whatever misgivings he had, he just couldn't pass up spending time with this woman. Somehow he knew if they went back to work now, he would be kicking himself later.

Neither of them said a word as he drove towards the heart of Boston. Other than making dinner plans, he hadn't mapped out an itinerary for them.

"Any favorite spots you'd like to visit? Faneuil Hall, the North End, Newbury Street? We have some time before dinner." Jake figured anyone could treat her to dinner at a restaurant; he wanted her to remember their time together. So instead of making a reservation at one of Boston's top notch restaurants, he'd arranged for a private dinner aboard a friend's yacht in the harbor. By sheer dumb luck the yacht had been in dry dock until two days earlier so it hadn't sustained any damage during the hurricane. Not that Boston Harbor had been damaged much anyway.

"Not really. I've never spent much time in Boston. Never had a real reason to, so whatever is fine."

The yacht's captain didn't expect them until five o'clock but if they arrived early he knew the man wouldn't complain. "In that case let's head over to the marina"

"The marina? Why are we going there?"

"You're just going to have to wait and see," Jake said as he headed in the direction of Boston Yacht Haven one of the city's most exclusive marinas.

I definitely owe Christopher one. Jake looked around as he followed Charlie through the yacht and onto the port side deck. His friend had made sure no detail was overlooked. The scent of several dozen flowers placed around the yacht filled the air. A romantic table for two stood prepared on the deck and a bottle of fine French wine sat on ice waiting for them. Since no other detail seemed overlooked he guessed his friend had also made sure the main sleeping cabin was prepared just in case Jake needed it.

Whatever favor Christopher called in later, it'd be worth it.

"When you said dinner I thought you meant at a restaurant downtown," Charlie said, her hazel eyes wide with astonishment as she took in her surroundings.

Jake pulled out Charlie's chair. "You can do that anytime. How often do you get to cruise around Boston Harbor at night and watch the sunset?"

"You've got me there," she admitted looking up at him, her lips turned up in a smile. "Is this your yacht?"

"No. It belongs to a friend of mine."

"He must be some friend."

"Christopher and I were roommates in college. We've been good friends ever since."

He couldn't keep himself from bending down and pressing his mouth against hers for what he intended to be a brief kiss. Soon the kiss turned hotter as she wrapped her arms around his neck and their tongues met.

Behind him Jake heard someone clear their throat. Pulling back, Jake stared down at Charlie, her eyes were closed and her lips were rosy from their kiss. Turning he looked at the woman who had interrupted them.

"The chef wants to know when you would like dinner served."

"Tell him we're ready whenever he is." Once they were alone again, he turned his attention back to Charlie. "I hope you are hungry. Christopher's chef is amazing." He let his hand linger on her shoulder. The skin beneath his hand was soft and he loathed the idea of losing the physical connection he had with her.

When her eyes fluttered open they locked onto his. The desire he saw in them matched his own. "I'm starved." She sounded breathless, and the cave man in him surged with pride because he knew he'd caused her current state of arousal.

"Did you always want to join the Navy?" The dinner plates were gone and they sat watching the final rays of sunshine disappear. The more they talked the more Jake wanted to know about Charlie. He'd been physically attracted to her from the first moment he saw her, but the more time he spent with her the more emotionally drawn to her he became. He found being around her intoxicating and hoped they could see each other after they both left Massachusetts.

Charlie shook her head without any hesitation. "I always wanted to be a doctor. Never even considered the Navy till I realized how expensive college and medical school were. A Navy recruiter came to my high school junior year and I knew that was the only way it would happen," she said, her voice a mixture of anger and sadness. "Even with scholarships I wouldn't have been able to swing it without a ridiculous amount of debt waiting for me at the end."

Jake could understand her reason. Even though he'd never worried about it, he knew education was expensive. "Do you ever regret your decision?"

"Nope. I got what I wanted and I'm serving my country. But that doesn't mean I want to be in the Navy forever," she said without pausing to consider her answer. "I keep going back and forth about staying. I finished filling out the paperwork, but it's still sitting in my room.

Must be nice not to have any regrets. He wouldn't mind trading places with her for a day or two. Although if he told her that, she'd probably fall off her chair laughing. Everyone thought he lived such a charmed life. No one ever stopped to think about how much a pain in the ass it could be with the media waiting for you to make a mistake.

"What about you? Did you always want to work for your family's company?"

"It wasn't anywhere on my radar." Jake heard the

bitterness in his voice but he couldn't keep it from creeping in. Although the foundation wasn't related to the hotel business, it was still tied to Sherbrooke Enterprises.

Charlie leaned forward, her interest obviously captured. "Really? What did you want to do?"

The last rays of sunshine danced across her hair and her astute gaze flickered over his face as if she could learn the answer on her own. And for some reason he sensed that perhaps she would truly understand; unlike anyone else he'd ever told.

"If you laugh I swear I'll toss you overboard," he threatened.

"I'm in the Navy, remember? I can swim."

Jake threw her a dirty look. "If that's the way you're going to be, forget it."

"All right. No laughing. Promise."

"I made up my mind when I was about twelve to go to the Naval Academy and be a SEAL. But it didn't happen."

Charlie's jaw dropped open and her eyebrows shot up. "You didn't get in?" Her voice rang with astonishment.

At least she didn't laugh. The last person he'd told laughed his ass off. "I didn't apply. My parents had other plans for me, and eventually I realized people would always wonder if I'd gotten in thanks to the family name."

The resentment he felt toward his parents whenever he thought about this crept through him. He loved them both and knew they loved him but their disappointment in the decisions he made cut him deep.

"They had it all figured out. My parents sent me to boarding school when I was fourteen. They wanted me to go to either Yale like my grandfather or Harvard like my father for undergrad and then Harvard for my MBA. After that I would join Sherbrooke Enterprises. And then eventually I'd transition into politics. That's been the basic life map for every Sherbrooke male for the past hundred years." Jake found the truth just spilled out as he spoke to Charlie. Unlike so many people he spent time with, he didn't feel as though he needed to omit details to protect himself.

The corners of her pale pink lips turned downward in a frown. "You went to boarding school at fourteen?"

"Choate Rosemary Hall in Connecticut. My father and grandfather went there too. My mom wanted me to go to Eton in England like Dylan but my father refused. I still remember the arguments they had over it."

"So which did you choose, Yale or Harvard?" Charlie reached across the table and took his hand.

"Neither. Went to Cal Tech. About as far away from an East Coast Ivy League school as I could get. Got my undergraduate and graduate degrees in engineering. Worked for an engineering firm out in LA for a few years before moving to Virginia."

Compassion and understanding spread across her face. Even though she hadn't said it, he knew that she understood why he'd made the decisions he had. Most people assumed he'd been rebelling against his parents, and to some extent he had. Yet there had been much more to his decisions than that. He'd been trying to prove to himself that he had some control over his future. That just because his last name was Sherbrooke he didn't have to follow the path so many in his family had.

"I left the engineering firm a few years ago to start the foundation." It was one of the only decisions he'd made as an adult that he was proud of.

"Do you ever regret not becoming a SEAL?" Sometime during his explanation she came to stand next to him and now she placed a reassuring hand on his face.

Jake averted his gaze and focused instead on the city skyline, "Every damn day."

Leaning closer she spoke in a tone filled with respect. "If you had, who knows what all those people your foundation helped would've done." Her voice dropped to almost a whisper. "And we might not have met."

Jake was floored by the feelings her words and gentle

touch evoked in him. They were so unfamiliar. Sure he'd desired plenty of women and enjoyed their company but he'd never felt such an emotional connection to one before. Of all the women he dated never had he confessed this regret. None of them had ever shown any interest. Most were more interested in what he could give them or what being seen with him meant. It didn't appear as if Charlie cared about either.

Pushing back his chair Jake pulled Charlie onto his lap. "I'm glad we did," he said before lightly kissing her. Like it had earlier, desire hot and heavy swept through his body the second his lips touched hers. When she wrapped her arms around his neck and wiggled her sexy bottom in order to get closer, he instantly became hard. Thoughts of tossing her over his shoulder and finding the closest bed ran through is mind. How would she react if he did?

Raising his mouth from hers, he kissed a path down her neck. "Do you want to see the rest of the yacht now? We didn't check out the bedrooms, or would you rather have dessert?" he asked his voice low and purposefully seductive.

"Depends, what is the chef planning?" Charlie asked with a trace of laughter in her voice. She didn't wait for an answer. Instead she slid off his lap giving Jake the only answer he needed.

Anticipation surged through him as Jake led her to the largest of the bedrooms below. Just as he expected, the room was prepared for them. The lights were dimmed and the sheets on the bed were neatly turned down.

"Where were we?" Charlie moved close to him and began to caress the back of his neck.

Rather than give her a verbal answer, he walked her backward and then eased her down onto the queen-sized bed. "Does right about here seem right?" He brushed his lips against hers as he spoke.

A soft moan escaped Charlie and she slipped a hand under his shirt searing a path up his back to his shoulders.

Not needing any further encouragement, Jake stood and pulled his shirt up over his head. Then he reached for Charlie's, intent on doing the same thing to hers. The sound of the beeping intercom on the wall halted his progress.

For half a heartbeat he stared at the offending box on the wall. "What the hell?" Slowly his brain registered what the sound was and stood.

This better be an emergency. With more force than necessary, Jake jabbed the talk button with his index finger. "Something wrong Captain?"

"I'm sorry to disturb you Mr. Sherbrooke. There is a disabled yacht just off our port. It's taking on water."

Frustrated Jake raked his fingers through his hair. "Get them on board and make sure you alert authorities. I'll be right up to greet them." Grabbing his shirt off the floor, he turned to Charlie who now sat upright on the bed. "We'll have to continue this another night," he said brushing his lips against hers one last time.

A devilish smile formed on her face. "I'm going to hold you to that."

***

By the middle of the following week more than half the town had power back and things were inching their way back to normal. Fewer and fewer people needed help every day, so Wednesday Charlie found herself helping her mom around the bed and breakfast. Two of the families who had been staying at the Victorian Rose left that morning and their rooms needed cleaning. Charlie doubted there would be paying guests anytime soon but the rooms still need to be prepared.

Working on autopilot she stripped the queen-sized bed in the Revere Room. Would she be getting Jake's room ready for a new guest soon too? With conditions in town improving she figured he wouldn't be sticking around much longer. He'd already been here a week and a half. How much longer would he feel the need to stay? Not once during their conversations did he mention how long he typically stayed in the field or when he planned on returning to Virginia. And they'd had plenty of talks since their dinner together the previous weekend. In fact he seemed to go out of his way to get time alone with her.

Charlie pulled the fitted sheet across the mattress and thought back over their talks. They seemed to discuss everything from books and music to sports and politics. They didn't always agree, but she found that she enjoyed their conversations and heated disagreements.

Their conversations weren't the only things she liked either. Charlie figured she could be kissed by Jake for the next hundred years and not tire of it. The man could kiss. She'd never considered herself a romantic, yet when his lips came in contact with hers it was like something out of a movie. Everything around her faded away. Warmth and tenderness swept through her body as a deep longing settled in her soul.

Charlie unconsciously sighed as she thought about the kiss they'd shared the night before. For the second straight night they'd both come down for a late night snack and ended up having homemade oatmeal cookies with a side make out session.

If your friends saw you now O'Brien, they'd think you'd been abducted by aliens. She didn't sigh and daydream about men. It simply wasn't her. Yet she was doing just that.

With more force than necessary she stuffed a pillow into a clean cotton pillow case. She prided herself on her ability to remain emotionally detached from the men she spent time with. No matter who she dated or became intimate with she always held back a part of herself. She never let her heart become invested in a relationship. It was the only sure way to avoid a broken heart.

This time things were different. Every day she found it a little more difficult to keep her emotions under lock and key. She kept trying to figure out why? Maybe if she knew why she could get a handle on it. Part of her wished she still thought of him as the spoiled playboy the media referred to as Prince Charming. Then she wouldn't have a problem keeping her heart safe. Though she still didn't know how much of his playboy status was fabricated by the media, he'd more than proven that he was more than just a spoiled rich guy. He cared about the welfare of others, no one could deny that.

Charlie tossed the pillow back onto the bed and reached for another. "I've got to get myself back in control." She stuffed the other pillow into its case.

Through the open bedroom window she heard a car pull into the gravel driveway. After a few minutes she heard the front door downstairs close. Despite her previous words to herself about getting back into control, hope and anticipation blossomed in her chest. Had Jake returned? He'd left right after breakfast. Lunch time had come and gone and he hadn't returned.

Determined not to look out the open window to see if his truck was back, Charlie spread the sage green comforter over the bed. "I've got issues," she said, her voice laced with annoyance and disgust. Turning from the bed she retrieved the bottle of Murphy's Oil Soap and the rag she'd brought up with her.

"You're not alone. We all have issues but talking to yourself can be a serious problem. You might want to see a professional," Jake said from the open doorway, the amusement in his voice apparent.

For a moment Charlie wanted to do something she'd never in her life done before; drop everything and run to the man leaning against the door frame and throw her arms around him. Instead she looked at him forcing her feet to stay rooted in place. "Can you suggest someone?"

"I've got a great shrink on speed dial. I'll give you the number."

He walked further into the room and Charlie swore the temperature jumped twenty degrees. *Doesn't he ever look unsightly like the rest of us mere mortals?* It just wasn't fair. No matter the time of day or what he'd been doing, Jake always looked incredibly sexy. Today was no exception. Wearing a pair of khaki Dockers and a light blue dress shirt with the sleeves rolled up he could've been a model in an ad for a weekend executive collection.

"Your mom said you were helping out. Almost done?" He wrapped his arms around her waist and pulled her close as he spoke. "Thought we'd head over to see Mr. Quinn."

All the nerves in Charlie's body quivered at the physical contact. It seemed no matter how many times he pulled her close like this it happened. Her entire body went on high alert with excitement and yearning.

Control. Somehow she needed to get a handle on these emotions. Otherwise she ran the risk of having her heart crushed. The last person who had done it was her father and she'd vowed it'd never happen again.

With that single word repeating in her head, she broke free then took a few steps away from him. "Give me another ten minutes and I'll be done. Dusting is all I have left. I'll meet you downstairs." She needed him to leave before she said the hell with dusting and threw her arms around him for one of his fabulous kisses.

Jake opened his mouth as if to say something but then closed it again. Stuffing his hands in his pockets he nodded. "I'll be in the kitchen getting a sandwich. I missed lunch."

Without another word he turned and headed back downstairs. He figured waiting in the kitchen was best. Being that close to her *and* a bed was dangerous. The minute he'd seen her in the bedroom he envisioned himself locking them in, peeling her clothes off and spending the rest of the day in bed getting to know every inch of her body, something he'd come close to doing on the yacht before their unexpected visitors arrived. In the middle of the day with her family around struck him as a bad time to give into his desires. He'd have to wait till they had more privacy, assuming her response on the boat hadn't been an isolated occurrence. He hoped it hadn't been.

Although the last thing he'd come here for was a relationship, Jake hoped she gave them a chance. Everything about her was so different from the women he normally dated, yet being with her felt right. Though they'd only known each other a short time, he felt like she understood him. She looked past his name and saw the man. True, at first she'd only seen what the media told everyone, but her opinion had changed. He could tell by the way she responded to his kisses and the way she spoke to him. When they first met she'd been indifferent and aloof. That wasn't the case anymore.

Thoughts about the first time they met were still running through his mind, when his cell phone rang. He knew from the ringtone it was his executive assistant, Cindy.

"Hi Cindy." Jake pulled out a chair at the kitchen table and made himself comfortable.

"How are things up there, Jake?"

Most executives would take exception to their employees calling them by their first name. In fact his father almost had a heart attack the first time he'd heard Cindy call him Jake. When he'd hired the fifty-something assistant he insisted that she call him Jake and not Mr. Sherbrooke. At first she balked at the idea, but after a while she complied. Now it sounded strange to hear her refer to him as anything other than Jake.

"Everything is coming along. A good portion of town has power back and our engineers have started plans for replacing the dam. I should be returning home soon."

"That's a relief. The place is falling apart without you."

Jake couldn't help but chuckle. Cindy ran a tight ship especially when he wasn't around so he knew there was no possibility of things falling apart without him. "I doubt that."

"You're right, no problems here. I called because I wanted to give you a heads up. Marcy Blake from Today magazine called looking for you this morning."

Every cell in Jake's body tensed up at the reporter's name. Whenever she called looking for a statement, it wasn't a good sign. The last time had been when news of Callie and Dylan's involvement had been made public.

"What did she want?" Jake leaned his forearms on the table prepared for bad news.

"She didn't say much. Only asked to speak with you. Maybe she's doing a piece on your sister's wedding next week," Cindy said sounding optimistic.

If it was any other reporter he would have agreed with his assistant's assumption, but not Marcy Blake. She was notorious for getting scandals out to her readers first, regardless of how accurate her facts were. She didn't care how her reporting the facts wrong affected people as long as the stories she wrote sold magazines and made her editors happy.

Unease settled in his gut, killing his appetite. He'd kept a low profile as of late so he couldn't think of any scandal she could link to him. Still if she called looking for him it wasn't a good sign. "Thanks for the heads up, Cindy. I'm sure she'll call my cell. It won't take that woman long to get her hands on my new number." He didn't know how she did it, but somehow she always managed to get her hands on his number. He'd changed it twice in the past two years for that very reason.

He was ending his conversation when Charlie walked in. "Cindy, I'll call you if I hear from Marcy. Let me know if anything comes up down there." Pushing the end button on the phone, he shoved it in his pocket and gave Charlie a smile. Though she smiled in return, it wasn't the same open inviting one she'd greeted him with earlier. This one was forced and her eyes reflected suspicion. He could tell she wanted to ask who he'd been talking to. For a moment he considered waiting to see if she would say anything, but in the end he decided to just come right out and tell her.

"That was my executive assistant Cindy. I don't know what I would do without her." Jake stood and moved toward her as he spoke. "Guess some reporter called looking for me today." Although it wasn't any of her business he didn't want to keep things from her. In his experience when you did that it often came back to bite you in the ass.

Some of the suspicion faded from her eyes, and she accepted his outstretched hand. "Maybe she heard about your work here and had a few questions."

Holding her hand, Jake led her toward the kitchen door. "She's not that kind of reporter. If it's not guaranteed to sell papers, she's not writing about it." Damn. He hated the Marcy Blake's of the world. "I'll find out what she wants soon enough, I'm sure," he said with resignation.

Jake didn't mention the reporter again though he couldn't shake the feeling that a scandal involving him or his family must be taking shape. Rather he focused his attention on Charlie and the Quinns. Once again when they arrived at the hospital they found Jessica with her grandparents. Much like his previous visits he talked to the family about everyday things and Mr. Quinn grilled him about the town's progress.

While Mr. Quinn shot questions at him, Charlie and Jessica used the time to catch up. He still found it odd that the two of them had been such good friends. They struck him as complete opposites especially considering their reaction the day of the accident. Charlie had remained calm and cool while Jessica had been almost hysterical. Yet he could see the close bond between the women as they talked. As he half-listened to Mr. Quinn explain his upcoming surgery, he listened to the conversation between the two old friends.

"You, Kate and I need to go out together the next time you come home. I don't think we have all hung out together since the summer after graduation," Jessica said.

"We've gone out since then." Jake noticed that when Charlie answered she looked everywhere but at her friend. "The summer I came home after freshman year."

Jessica shook her head. "You and I went out. Kate didn't come. And we have not been out since. The day grandpa fell was the first time I'd seen you in years. I didn't even know you were home. You should visit Kate before you leave. Did you know she has two kids now?"

Once again he wondered how long it'd been since Charlie's last visit home. From the previous conversations he'd overheard and what they were saying now, it seemed as if it'd been awhile. Why was that? True, being a doctor in the Navy wasn't a nine-to-five job with vacation time you could take without advance planning, but that didn't mean she didn't have some leave every year. She seemed to get along with her family so why not come home more often?

Whether or not she sees her family isn't any of my business. He often went long stretches between seeing his parents too.

"Doc says I'll need a chair for a while. Physical therapy too," Mr. Quinn grumbled interrupting Jake's thoughts. "Who has time for that? Who's going to run the store?"

Jake tried to hide his smile as he watched Mrs. Quinn pat her husband's hand.

"Jess practically runs the place now and you know it. You just don't want to do the therapy."

Mr. Quinn snatched his hand away from his wife, his bright red face giving away his embarrassment. The way Jake figured it, the guy had nothing to be embarrassed about. The woman clearly loved him and didn't have any qualms about giving him a hard time. It was just what he wanted someday. The right woman just hadn't come along yet.

Thinking back over the relationships he'd been in, his

eyes moved to where Charlie sat. She was explaining the importance of physical therapy to the Quinns, but it wasn't her words that drew Jake's attention. Rather it was her tone. Though she was straightforward and blunt, her voice was compassionate. Her hazel eyes were warm and caring. There didn't seem to be anything fake or contrived about her. With Charlie what you saw was what you got. It was such a change from the women he normally found himself attracted to. And he suspected it was that very quality about her that had him wanting to get to know her better. Something he hoped would happen next weekend, if she agreed to accompany him.

He'd been mulling over the idea since last night. One minute inviting her seemed like a fabulous idea; the next it struck him as a disaster waiting to happen. Most of the time he wasn't so indecisive, he didn't know why he was this time. It wasn't like another guest would be a big deal. After all more than three hundred people were already expected. Still Jake straddled the fence tipping back and forth like a see-saw.

About an hour later he walked with Charlie out to the parking lot. Like they always did when he left, the Quinns had thanked him for everything and had extended an invitation for dinner at their house once Mr. Quinn left the hospital.

"I think you've got some new admirers." Laughing Charlie reached for the SUV's door handle.

Darting his hand out before she could grip the handle, Jake pulled the door open for her with one hand while he wrapped his other around her forearm anchoring her next to him. If she really wanted to she could move, but the slight touch kept her beside the SUV.

"I can see myself being a bit like Mr. Quinn someday."

The corners of Charlie's mouth curved upward. "You're going to be a hardware store owner with a broken hip when you grow up?" she asked with a gleam in her eye.

Jake tugged on her arm until she was standing close

enough for him to see the flecks of green in her hazel eyes. Focusing on her lips he lowered his head toward her, stopping when they were mere inches apart. Finally, he could do what he'd wanted to do since they exited the hospital.

"I meant a stubborn old man who doesn't like sitting around on his ass." He didn't give her a chance to comment. Instead he took her lips in a slow tender kiss, one that he intended to tease her with. They'd shared several passionate kisses, but he was always the aggressor. This time he wanted her to control things. Well at least as far as this kiss was concerned. He wanted to see how heated their kiss would be if he didn't keep kicking it up a notch.

Charlie didn't keep him waiting long. She ran her tongue along the seam of his lips enticing him to open for her. When he didn't comply she pressed her body against his, crushing her breasts against his chest and tugging on his bottom lip with her mouth.

Unable to help himself, Jake succumbed to her tactics. Like always she tasted like mint. Whether it was her toothpaste or some candy she favored, he didn't know. But he knew that he was never going to be able to taste mint again without thinking of Charlotte O'Brien.

Jake looped his arms around Charlie's waist and lost himself in their kiss. All thoughts of Mr. Quinn and their visit evaporated as did any thoughts of where they were. His first pull back to reality came in the form of a car's horn. It blared as it passed down the side street near the parking lot. A wolf whistle followed the offensive sound and caused Jake to pull back just in time to see a car pass by.

"I think that's our cue to leave." He pulled back enough to look Charlie in the face and he felt Charlie's hands leave his shoulders.

"We seem to be making a habit out of this. Maybe we should find a better place next time," she said before climbing into the passenger seat

I couldn't agree more. In that moment he made up his mind about asking her to accompany him that weekend.

CHAPTER 5

"You want me to what?" Charlie knew she sounded like an idiot, yet she couldn't help it. Maybe she needed to have her hearing checked. Jake couldn't have just asked what she thought he did.

Jake leaned his shoulder against the door frame near the stairs heading up to the attic, his arms crossed over his chest. Everyone at the bed and breakfast was gathered downstairs waiting to eat. Everyone except them. She'd gone upstairs to check her cell phone messages and when she came down Jake stood leaning against the wall waiting for her.

"Come with me to Newport this weekend. I'm the best man. It wouldn't be right for me to show up without a date."

Okay, maybe she hadn't misunderstood. "Isn't that what the single bridesmaids are for?" Charlie walked down the last few steps stopping in front of him. Sure they'd shared some amazing kisses but going to his sister's wedding was out there. Especially this wedding. The media was calling it *the* wedding of the year.

Shrugging Jake gave her a lazy smile. "One's my sister, Sara, and the others just don't do it for me."

She wanted to ask him what he meant by 'do it' but if the way he looked at her was any indication, she didn't have to. A heady combination of desire and curiosity sprang to life. The men she came in contact with on a daily basis never looked at her the way Jake was. Most viewed her as nothing more than a doctor and Naval officer, they seemed to overlook the fact that she was also a woman. Jake's red-hot gaze told her that he not only noticed that she was a woman, but that he wanted her. And the attraction wasn't one-sided. She wanted him with a ferocity that she'd never experienced before.

"We'll only be gone a few days." As he spoke, Jake straightened and closed the gap between them. "You can meet my family. I think you'll like them."

Afraid he'd see the uncertainty she felt, Charlie looked at everything but Jake. She wasn't worried about how long they'd be gone. Nobody really needed her here. Every day the town recovered a little more and, as always, her mom had her brother Sean; she didn't need anyone else. That was part of the reason she came home so infrequently. Rather she worried Jake might get the wrong idea if she accepted the invitation. He may begin to think she wanted a long-term relationship, and she didn't. Relationships that had the possibility of a future were not in the cards for her. She decided that a long time ago.

Get over yourself Charlie; this is Jake Sherbrooke world-renowned playboy. He's not interested in a relationship. Charlie's inner thoughts helped bring her back to reality. Although he'd shown that he wasn't just another rich son living off the family's money, he did still have a reputation for leaving behind many broken hearts.

This is the wedding of the year, she reminded herself. The media had been talking about it for months. Attending it was a once-in-a-lifetime opportunity. She could picture the expressions on her friends' faces if she told them she went. Not to mention Newport was beautiful this time of year. Somehow the hurricane that devastated North Salem by destroying the Stonefield Dam had left the town of Newport and most of Rhode Island unscathed.

"You're tempted," Jake said. "I promise no one there will bite." Dropping his head he nibbled on her ear lobe. "It'll give us some time alone together."

Before she could stop herself, Charlie sighed in pleasure. His teasing only increased the throbbing sensation in her body. Much more of it and she might ask him upstairs for a bit to pick up where they'd left off the previous weekend.

"Okay. But only because this is *the* wedding of the year. It has nothing to do with you." Somehow she managed to tease him while maintaining a straight face.

Jake broke off his assault and straightened to his full height. For a minute he studied her and Charlie was positive she saw a flash of insecurity flicker across his face. Just as quickly, however, his lips curved into a smile and she wondered if she'd imagined it.

"That so, Doc? Then I'll just have to work extra hard to change that."

***

Jake almost wanted to whistle as he got dressed, his mood was that good. Everything was going well. Progress in town was coming along and Charlie had agreed to go to Newport with him for the weekend. Now that he'd asked, he wondered why he'd struggled with the decision at all. As soon as he said the words, he'd known it was the right choice.

He hadn't come to North Salem looking for a date, yet he couldn't deny the attraction he felt toward her. He knew it wasn't one-sided either. Being together this weekend would give them time to explore that attraction. At the same time, having her as a date would keep at least some of the single socialites at the wedding away from him.

Before heading down for coffee Jake grabbed his cell

off the nightstand. A quick glance at the screen told him he'd missed two calls, one from his half-sister Callie and another from Marcy Blake, aka the reporter from hell. Both callers left messages. Jake didn't bother to listen to the message from Marcy, but he did check Callie's. He'd only met Callie the year before, but in that short time they'd developed a strong bond. In fact he often forgot that she was only his half-sister. In truth he got along as well with her as he did with his full sister Sara, and they'd grown up together. So when he heard Callie's message and she said it was important that he call her back, he didn't hesitate.

Jake listened as the phone rang several times.

"Jake, hold on a sec," an out of breath Callie said after the fifth ring.

"Sure thing," he replied although he didn't know if she'd heard him. While he waited he decided to get comfortable on the padded window seat.

"Sorry about that. Problems with the florist," Callie said coming back on the phone a minute later.

"No worries. What's up? Your message said it was important." Whatever it was it had to be big. Final preparations for the wedding kept her busy so she wouldn't just call him on a whim.

On the other end of the line it sounded as if Callie sighed. "I got a call from Marcy Blake this morning. Have you talked to her?"

At the sound of the reporter's name the dread he'd felt the day before returned. Something was up; there was no doubt about it. Not only had the reporter called him, but she contacted his family too. Not a good sign.

"No but she's called the office and my cell." Jake paused, afraid to ask what the reporter wanted. Mentally he did an inventory of all his recent activities and relationships. Not a single thing stood out as being of any interest to this reporter. "What did she want?"

"Are you sitting down?" Callie asked her voice laced

with concern.

Half a dozen curses went through Jake's head. He wasn't going to like whatever his sister had to say. "Spit it out Callie."

Another sigh came through the phone, this one louder than before. "She wanted to know how the family felt about you becoming a father. And whether or not you and Blair were discussing wedding plans now that you're expecting."

Jake laughed aloud. His sister's statement was absurd. Anyone else and he'd think they were joking, but he knew Callie wouldn't joke about something like this.

"Is it true? Are you guys having a baby? I thought you broke things off with her." Callie sounded confused.

"Hell no! I ended things with Blair more than two months ago. I broke up with her when I got back from London. Besides we always used protection." When the reporter started calling he knew it meant trouble, but he'd never expected this. Sure Blair was upset when he ended things, and she had tried to convince him to give her another chance, but he hadn't pegged her as a vengeful woman. A little shallow and conceited perhaps but not someone capable of being malicious.

"What did you tell her?" He knew Callie wouldn't intentionally say anything to make the situation worse, but she was still learning how to handle the media vultures.

"The truth. I told her I didn't know what she was talking about. I'm not sure that she believed me though."

It wasn't a matter of whether or not Marcy Blake believed Callie. Rather it was what story would sell the most magazines. A story about him becoming a father would sure be a hit. Damn it. He'd managed to avoid negative publicity for months and now this had to surface just days before his sister's wedding. "Has she called anyone else?" He didn't need a lecture from his father.

"I don't think so. Dylan's been in Japan, he's coming home tonight. I haven't heard from anyone else."

Callie sounded worried and Jake could picture her nibbling on her bottom lip like she always did when something bothered her. With the wedding only a few days away she had enough to worry about. He didn't want her thinking about this too.

"Thanks for the heads up. I'll take care of it. Don't worry. Go straighten out whatever problem you've got with the flowers. I don't want to have to pick flowers from the garden for you on Saturday."

"Honestly, I'm tempted to let your mother deal with it. I think the florist is afraid of her."

Jake didn't doubt it. A good recommendation from Elizabeth Sherbrooke, and the florist's business would sky rocket. At the same time a bad one and his business could go down the proverbial drain.

"You won't do that and you know it."

"You're right, but it is so tempting. She'd have everything straightened out in no time."

"All done with the seating arrangement?"

Callie groaned on the other end. "Don't ask."

"Then you won't mind adding one more guest. I'm coming with a date. Someone I met up here." Jake told his sister a little about Charlie before hanging up. Once he was done with his conversation, Jake remained sitting and stared out the window.

What the hell was Blair up to? Was she really that pissed? Sure he'd known she was angry but this was going a bit far. And what did she hope to accomplish? If she was pregnant did she expect him to marry her? Maybe if it was his kid, he'd consider it but there was no way it could be. He'd broken up with her more than two months ago and before that he'd been in England for a solid month. Their final month together as a couple they'd hardly ever seen each other. She'd spent most of that month out in California visiting family and he'd been in Virginia. Between all that time apart and the fact that they always used protection he didn't believe it was possible for her to be pregnant with his child.

In the driveway below he saw Charlie walking towards her car. Dressed in a navy blue t-shirt and denim shorts that showed off her lean shapely legs, she walked with her head held high and her back perfectly straight. What were her plans this morning? He'd hoped to see her before he headed over to the town hall to check on repairs. It didn't look like that was going to happen now.

As he continued to watch, she climbed into her car and drove away. So much for his good mood. Jake watched as the car disappeared from sight. Suddenly reluctant to start his day, Jake came to his feet. He had people waiting for him and a new scandal brewing. This was not the time for sitting around.

***

Once again Charlie found herself volunteering to play babysitter at the shelter while homeowners worked to get their lives back together. Thankfully several families had already left the shelter. They'd either made arrangements with other family members or found places to stay outside of town so there were fewer children around today. Despite the reduced number, Charlie still felt as if she'd landed on an alien planet. She just wasn't used to being around this many children all at once. She hoped the children didn't know how uncomfortable she was. Who knew how they might take advantage of her if they did.

"Can you help me? The eyes won't stick," a young girl with curly blond hair asked holding up a pair of googly eyes.

Somehow she'd been left to supervise the craft table again that morning. Charlie looked at the paper bird set out on the table and back at the young girl who looked familiar. Not wanting to disappoint the little girl, she picked up the glue bottle and prepared to tackle the problem.

"Try using regular glue instead." Charlie squirted two drops of Elmer's onto the paper bird's face. "It might work better than those glue sticks."

The little girl smiled up at her, reminding Charlie of an old classmate. "Is your dad Don Sullivan?"

The girl nodded her head causing the blond curls to bounce wildly about her face. "People call him Donnie. They call my brother that too. They have the same name," the little girl answered as she proceeded to color the feathers on her bird now that it had eyes.

Donnie had children? Wow! Now there was a shocker. She couldn't even picture him with a woman. In school he'd been the geeky nerd the other kids turned to when they needed help with their algebra. As far as she knew he never even had a date in high school. He'd taken his third cousin to the senior prom, though he refused to admit it. Obviously he had changed since then.

"This is a present for mom and dad," the little girl said holding up her bird. "They can hang it up when we go home."

Charlie stared at the lopsided bird with the googly eyes and colorful feathers unsure of what to say. How much did the girl understand? Did she know they might never return to the home she'd once known? She didn't know what damage her former classmate's house had suffered but if the family was still at the shelter it must be significant.

"I'm sure they'll love it. Do you want me to write a message on it?" Charlie forced herself to smile.

The girl handed her a purple marker. "Love, Ellie."

Charlie printed the words on the belly of the bird and handed it back.

"Thanks," the girl said before sprinting off toward other children.

With the departure of the little girl the craft table was empty and Charlie began to clean up the scraps of paper left behind. She tried not to think about the children playing tag further down the room. It was bad enough that the adults had lost everything but at least they understood. The children didn't. She'd overheard them talking and many seemed to think they'd be going home any day now; back to the homes they'd always lived in. It just wasn't fair. Children deserved a chance to grow up without worries or loss. There would be enough opportunities for that when they grew up. They shouldn't have to face it now.

Life isn't always fair. Charlie knew that first hand. If it was, her father wouldn't have walked out on her and Sean. Regardless these children would survive their loss just as she had. It might not be easy, then again few things in life were.

Like the old saying went, what doesn't kill you only makes you stronger? As far as Charlie was concerned, truer words had never been spoken.

After she finished cleaning up the craft supplies, Charlie crossed to the other side of the room where Lizzie was organizing a game of musical chairs. It looked as if Lizzie needed some help as she tried to explain the rules of the game to a group of children. From the expressions on their faces, Charlie guessed that they had never played before. She'd never considered musical chairs a complicated game, but the confused expressions on the children's faces told her that was strictly a matter of opinion. Just like everything else in life. "Do you want me to try explaining it?" Charlie asked.

***

"Thanks for coming with me," Charlie said pulling into the Hamilton Mall parking lot the next afternoon. With the wedding in Newport only two days away she needed something to wear.

"I'm glad you asked," Jessica answered. "I still can't believe Jake Sherbrooke asked you to be his date. Are you nervous?"

Charlie ran through a mental inventory of her emotions. Nervousness about meeting his family hovered around the edges of her mind while anticipation all but consumed her. Since the night on the yacht, Jake hadn't made any attempt at intimacy, yet she expected it to happen this weekend.

"It's only a wedding." Charlie pulled open the door to Macy's.

Jessica stopped dead in her tracks, her eyes wide and her lips parted in surprise. "How can you say that? It's all the media is talking about. Hollywood stars and multimillionaires are going to be there. Not to mention Jake Sherbrooke is your date."

"I didn't say I wasn't excited. Just that I'm not all that nervous," Charlie answered with quiet emphasis. "Now are you going to help me find a dress or not?"

Jessica began moving again. "Are we looking for something blue or is that not your favorite color anymore?"

"Jake said the bridesmaids are wearing royal blue so unfortunately I need to pick something else."

"Too bad you don't like yellow. Supposedly it's the in color this season."

A sense of guilt pressed down on Charlie as she watched Jessica stroll between the racks of dresses. In high school they'd been the closest of friends. Over the years though she'd made little effort to stay in contact, yet Jessica still remembered what colors she preferred. Now that she had reconnected with Jessica she wouldn't let that happen again. When she returned to Virginia she would make an effort to keep in touch.

Charlie pushed the guilt away and stopped at a rack of dresses. "What do you think of this one?" Charlie held up a simple black cocktail dress.

"You can't wear black to an afternoon wedding." Jessica grabbed the dress out of Charlie's hands and held up a floor length lilac gown. "This one would work though."

It took them several tries but after two hours of shopping they agreed on a strapless cream-colored floor length gown with an open back. With Jessica's help Charlie choose a pair of silver heels and a silver clutch that matched the silver beading around the sweetheart neckline.

With the purchases in the car, Charlie pulled onto the highway. "Thanks for your help. I would've ended up with that black dress if it wasn't for you."

"Any time, Charlie. You have to come in when you drop me off. I have some jewelry that'll go perfectly with that dress."

CHAPTER 6

Of all of the absurd things she'd done, this one topped the list. According to the media this was *the* wedding. Even her friends, who like her didn't care about the actions of the rich and famous, had been talking about this wedding for months. And it was hard not to. The President's formerly unknown illegitimate daughter was marrying billionaire CEO Dylan Talbot who just happened to be the President's stepson.

Charlie couldn't help but think that she shouldn't be going. She had no ties to the family and had only known Jake for a couple of weeks. Yet even though she planned to tell Jake she'd changed her mind, each time she tried she couldn't bring herself to do it. How often did someone like her get to attend a wedding like this?

The prospect of seeing the wedding wasn't the only thing that held Charlie back from canceling. Though she hated to admit it, she was looking forward to spending a few days away with Prince Charming as the media like to call him. She knew he would be returning to Virginia soon. While the town wasn't yet back to normal, everything continued to improve and the day-to-day recovery operations didn't require Jake's attention. Besides who

80

knew when his foundation's help would be needed elsewhere.

When he left she'd miss him. While they didn't live that far apart in Virginia they didn't exactly travel in the same circles. The likelihood of them seeing each other again was remote, which shouldn't have bothered her. Or at least she kept telling herself that as she packed.

You've got to get your head on straight. Enjoy your time with him but don't get attached. Once he leaves, that's it. Chances are he won't even remember your name.

A wave of sadness crashed over her at the thought of him forgetting her. Charlie knew she wouldn't forget him or the kisses they'd shared. Then again she didn't have gorgeous men throwing themselves at her feet left and right. Jake on the other hand had no shortage of women looking to spend time with him. Though he'd downplayed the number of relationships he'd been in, Charlie didn't doubt the number still far surpassed her not insignificant total.

Charlie balled up a t-shirt and shoved it into her bag, then zipped it closed. Damn that hurricane. It had upset more than just the town. It'd even managed to wreak havoc on her usually well-controlled emotions.

From now on she was going to keep her emotions in check. No longer would it bother her that Jake would soon be just a pleasant memory that she could share with her friends when she got home. With her mind made up she pulled the bag off the bed and headed downstairs.

***

Somebody needs to wake me. Charlie fidgeted in the front seat, her stomach churning with anxiety as Jake drove the Escalade through the security gate at Cliff House. Before she could stop herself she turned to look out the back window as the gate closed, keeping out any unwanted visitors including the numerous news vans parked on the street.

"I can't believe the reporters are here already," Charlie

said turning back around. "The wedding isn't until tomorrow afternoon."

Jake reached over and took hold of her hand. Charlie knew he could feel how clammy it was yet he didn't comment. Thank God. Just having him know she was nervous embarrassed her. She didn't need him commenting on it too.

"They've probably been here all week. Imagine the disaster it would be if those vultures missed something." Jake's tone told her all she needed to know about how he viewed the reporters.

After traveling down a long winding driveway, Jake pulled into a garage bigger than her house and filled with expensive cars. At the far end sat a black Aston Martin and next to it was a bright red Ferrari.

"Did you tell your family you were bringing a guest?" Butterflies took off in her stomach at the thought of meeting the owners of the cars parked around them.

"I told Callie. I'm sure she told everyone else." Jake pulled the keys out of the ignition but didn't make any move to get out. "Don't tell me the doctor is nervous?"

Charlie licked her dry lips and looked everywhere but at him. She never suffered attacks of nervousness, yet a mammoth butterfly fluttered around in her stomach now.

Reaching out Jake cupped the side of her face. "You shouldn't be nervous. My family is a little annoying but generally harmless."

A sarcastic laugh escaped Charlie. "Your father is the President of the United States. He's the most powerful man in the world. I wouldn't call him harmless."

Jake shrugged and threw her a carefree grin. "Don't worry Doc, I'll protect you. Promise." Without hesitating he leaned closer and sealed his promise with a gentle kiss. A kiss that turned from gentle to hungry and urgent in the blink of an eye.

Man that guy kisses like nobody's business. Charlie didn't want to think about all the practice he must have had to get that incredible. If she did, the ugly jealousy monster would begin to make an appearance again. Jealousy wasn't a rational emotion and definitely not one she had any right to feel.

Charlie knew the minute he decided to end the kiss. There was a subtle change in the pressure of his lips. It was always that way. For a moment she toyed with the idea of trying to get him to continue his heavenly onslaught. More than once she'd been able to do it. But today she doubted she'd be able to.

"I'd love to stay here with you all day, but they'll be wondering where we are. The Secret Service will have let them know we've arrived."

Charlie nodded, not wanting to speak. If she did, Jake would know just how breathless his kiss left her and she didn't see any need to stroke the guy's ego.

"Just relax. Everything will be fine. You're going to have a great weekend."

Jake didn't wait for a reply; instead he opened his car door.

"Enjoy yourself and think of all the stories you'll be able to tell people later," she said under her breath as she waited for Jake to open her car door. A few weeks earlier she would have done it herself, but since spending time in his company she'd gotten used to him opening doors for her. While she'd never admit it to anyone, she liked having him do it. It made her feel pampered and special. When they parted ways she would miss these unfamiliar feelings. *I'm not going to focus on that now. This weekend is all about having some fun.* Jake reached for her hand and they walked out of the garage and into the bright sunshine together.

They hadn't even made it out of the grand marble-tiled foyer with its pillars and vaulted ceiling when a petite woman with long mahogany hair and eyes identical to Jake's greeted them. Charlie may not read popular celebrity magazines often, but even she recognized Callie Taylor, Jake's half-sister. She'd thought the woman was pretty when she'd seen her in photos but they didn't do her justice. It was no wonder Dylan Talbot had fallen in love with her.

Jake enveloped the petite woman in a warm hug making it clear to Charlie just how much he cared about her. When was the last time Sean hugged her like that? The question popped into Charlie's head out of nowhere. Her brother never showed his emotions, even when they were younger. He didn't hug but rather gave a slap on the back. Watching Jake with his sister sent her back through her memories searching for the last time Sean had given her a hug even remotely close to the one Jake shared with Callie. It'd been right after their parents' divorce when she'd realized her dad wasn't coming home. Sean had hugged her as she cried and he promised that everything would be fine. Up till that day she had secretly hoped her dad still might come home even though he'd been gone a year. That somehow things would go back to the way they were before he walked out on them without even saying goodbye. Yet when her mom and Sean returned home from the courthouse that afternoon, she'd known life would never be the same.

"This is Charlotte."

Jake's words pulled her away from her memories and back to the marble foyer.

"You've probably guessed already, but this is my sister and the bride-to-be, Callie."

Charlie smiled. "Nice to meet you." Extending her hand she waited for the other woman to take it but instead Callie stepped toward her and hugged her. Taken back Charlie stood frozen for half a second before returning the warm gesture.

"I'm glad you could come. Someone needs to make sure my brother behaves himself," Callie said nodding in Jake's direction. In a flash the smile that had been on Callie's face faded. "Warren wants to see you."

By the way Callie looked over at Jake, Charlie guessed

he already knew what his father wanted

"I'll keep Charlotte company."

Despite his sister's reassurance Jake still didn't move. Something was up. Jake always spoke warmly about his family, giving her the impression that they were a tight-knit group, so his current reluctance didn't make a lot of sense.

Mind your own business. If he wants to share he will, Charlie told herself.

"Go ahead. I'll be fine." Charlie took a step away from him.

Jake watched as his sister led Charlie away. "Do you like baseball?" He heard his sister ask as the women walked up the grand staircase.

At least someone will have a good afternoon. Jake turned toward the hall that led to his father's study. Callie was one of the friendliest people he knew. If anyone could make Charlie feel comfortable here, it was her. Why couldn't his father have waited for this? He knew his father wanted to discuss the Blair situation. A situation he was already handling. He didn't need his family getting involved. Although he'd expected their interference, he'd hoped they'd wait till after the wedding. They knew he had a guest with him.

Standing in front of his father's study, he paused. Right now he should be the one showing Charlie around. Maybe they could have hid out on the sail boat he kept moored here for some private time before lunch. She'd told him she was eager to give sailing a try. But instead of doing that he was about to face the firing squad.

Hell.

Raising his fist, he knocked on the heavy mahogany door and waited. From the other side his father told him to come in. Taking another deep breath, he turned the knob and entered.

The familiar scent of old books and leather enveloped him. He'd always loved this room. Other than his own private suite on the second floor overlooking the ocean, this was his favorite room at Cliff House. As usual his father sat behind his massive antique desk, a mug of coffee and several documents in front of him. On the other side of the desk in one of the leather chairs sat his half-brother Dylan.

"About time my best man got here," Dylan greeted. Coming to his feet he smiled and gave Jake a thump on the back.

Jake couldn't remember ever seeing his brother as happy as he'd been during the past year and today was no exception. "Wouldn't miss it for the world. Just don't forget you wouldn't even be getting married if it wasn't for me. You owe me one." Jake couldn't resist giving his brother a hard time.

"I'll be sure to return the favor if the need ever arises," Dylan replied with all seriousness.

Jake saw his father take off his reading glasses, a signal that he was ready to get down to business. Cursing under his breath he took the other seat in front of the desk. "None of it's true," he said before anyone else could say a word.

"Are you sure? You were with Blair for several months. Accidents happen."

No kidding? Really? Wasn't Callie proof of that? Jake wanted to say but held back. Being a wise ass toward his father wasn't going to help with anything. "She'd have to be at least four months pregnant for it to be mine. I ran into her a few weeks ago and there's no way Blair is that pregnant." Jake shifted in his seat. Even though he was an adult he still found it uncomfortable to discuss his sex life with his father. With his brother it was one thing, but it didn't feel right with his father.

"Are you sure about that? Could you be confused about the dates?" his father asked.

Jake heard Dylan cover up a half laugh with a fake cough and threw him a dirty look. "I ended things with her over 2 months ago and before that I was in England for over a month. You know she didn't come with me." Even if it'd been a normal trip he wouldn't have taken Blair, but this trip had been anything but typical. "Before I left we hadn't been spending a lot of time together. Besides we always used something." Though he hadn't ended things with her until coming back, he'd known their relationship wasn't working before he left for England.

How could he have been so wrong about Blair? He'd known she wasn't *the* woman for him, but he never would have guessed she'd pull this stunt.

"I see. Have you spoken to her? Any idea why she's coming at you like this?"

Jake watched as his father drummed his finger tips on the desk telling him he was deep in thought trying to examine the problem from all aspects.

"Damned if I know." He raked a hand through his hair. "We talked recently and she didn't mention a thing to me then. She just asked me to meet her in New York for the weekend. I already called my lawyer." Jake wanted his father to know he was already on top of things.

"What did he say?" Dylan asked.

"He's pushing for an ultrasound and DNA testing."

"I want to get Marty and our lawyers involved with this. They should be able to get this mess cleared up before it does too much damage to the family."

More than anything he wanted to avoid having the family's team of lawyers and Marty Phillips involved in this. There was no denying that Marty Phillips knew what he was doing. Jake didn't like him, especially not after the way he'd treated Callie the year before. And while the lawyers that worked for Sherbrooke Enterprises were some of the best around, he had full confidence in his own hand-picked lawyer.

"No. Don't get them involved. I will take care of this problem."

When his father didn't immediately respond, Jake

assumed he was preparing his counter argument. Not that it would do any good. He'd already made up his mind and nothing his father said would change it.

"Are you positive? They'll be able to get things to happen quicker." Warren leaned back in his chair.

"I've got this one, Dad." Jake said in tone that let his father and brother know he was done discussing the situation.

"Callie told me you brought a date," Dylan said changing the topic of their conversation. "You must have just met her. Last time we talked you planned on flying solo."

Jake didn't miss the curiosity in his half-brother's voice or the raised eyebrow his father threw in his direction. He could imagine the questions floating around in his father's head. Though Dylan knew he wasn't the player the media made him out to be, his father didn't.

"Met her in North Salem. Her family runs the bed and breakfast where I've been staying."

"What do you know about her?" his father asked, reaching for his coffee.

It was a valid question especially considering the current situation with his ex, but it still irked him. Who he spent his time with was no one's business but his.

"She's a Navy doctor stationed in Virginia. And I should save her from Callie before she bores her to death with wedding details." Jake came to his feet and started to walk toward the door, pleased that he could use this opportunity to get away from the grilling and back to Charlie. "I'll see you both at the rehearsal dinner," he called over his shoulder before heading off in search of Charlie and his sister.

***

The view from the guest bedroom reminded her of something out of a movie. Actually everything in Cliff House looked as if it belonged either on some classic movie set or in a museum. Antique furniture filled the rooms. Priceless paintings hung in gilded frames on the walls and marble fireplaces were located in each room.

Although she'd grown up in New England and had visited Newport a few times, she'd never toured any of the mansions that lined Bellevue Avenue. Before today she'd only seen pictures of these American castles and none had really prepared her for being inside one of these magnificent homes built by the ultra wealthy of the 19th century as summer cottages.

"If I had a view like this, I'd never leave," Charlie said. She, Callie and Callie's best friend Lauren sat on the balcony off Charlie's room drinking freshly brewed iced tea. As Jake had predicted she really liked his half-sister. She was friendly and down to earth. Charlie suspected that might be partially because she hadn't grown up in the world of the super rich.

Callie nodded, a smile spread across her heart-shaped face. "I agree. I have trouble leaving every time I come."

"I think the only reason she does leave is because Mrs. Sherbrooke doesn't allow her and Dylan to share a bedroom when she's around," Lauren said refilling her glass.

"Seriously?"

Callie nodded. "Elizabeth doesn't like Dylan and me to share a room when she's here. She's a little old-fashioned sometimes. That's why you have your own room this weekend. But don't worry Jake's just down the hall."

Trying not to be obvious, Charlie glanced at her watch. More than an hour had passed since Jake left her to meet with his father, and although she was comfortable in Callie's company she wondered what kept him.

"They'll probably be done soon." Callie picked up her glass of iced tea. "Dylan and Warren both know you're here."

No sooner did Callie speak the words than Jake walked in. Charlie could tell something was bothering him the second she saw him. The easy-going smile that usually graced his face was gone and had been replaced with a somber look. Whatever his father wanted to see him about had obviously upset him.

"Not sure I like the looks of this. What stories have you been telling her about me Callie?" Jake walked over and dropped into the cushioned chair next to hers.

Though he tried to keep his voice light and carefree it sounded strained to her, and she couldn't help but try to cheer him up with a little teasing. "Who said we're talking about you. I know you find it hard to believe, but you're not the only man in the world. Callie was telling me about a friend she has coming to the wedding and she thinks he's perfect for me. She's going to introduce us so we can dance." Though her teasing statement lacked much originality she hoped it would at least elicit a laugh from him. Instead it seemed to have the opposite effect as a stormy look of anger passed over his face.

"Don't think so Doc. I've already filled up your dance card for tomorrow."

She wanted to come back with a sassy reply, but she didn't have one. A blank slate now occupied her mind. She wasn't used to men being possessive of her actions. With anyone else, she knew she would resent it. For some reason though, Charlie didn't find the comment offensive coming from him. *He's just playing around too. And you did open yourself up for it.*

In the end though it didn't matter that she didn't have a smart comeback because Callie changed the topic of the conversation to Jake's work in North Salem. While she could have added to the discussion, Charlie remained silent, only speaking when Jake or Callie directed a question her way. By doing so she got an up close and personal look at Jake with his family. Something she guessed few people got.

"Before I forget, the Marshalls are coming," Callie said after Jake finished answering her question about recovery efforts.

Charlie assumed this was somehow significant because the second the words left Callie's mouth Jake groaned.

"All of them or just Richard and Janet?"

"All. Sorry. Your mom insisted we couldn't leave them out."

Charlie glanced from Callie to Jake and finally Lauren who was attempting to stifle a laugh. "What's wrong with the Marshalls?"

"What isn't?" Jake replied.

Callie tossed her brother a dirty look and then answered. "Richard and Warren grew up together and have stayed close. He and his wife aren't the problem. Evidently their youngest daughter has always had a thing for my brother. When they were all here for New Year's Eve she wouldn't leave him alone."

"More like she stalked me all night, even though I had a date."

"How old is she?" The person in question must be very young. She envisioned an infatuated fifteen year old following Jake around the ballroom.

"A little younger than Sara, right?" Callie looked over at Jake for confirmation.

Jake slumped back in his chair and put his feet up on the railing. "Yeah. I think she's twenty-two."

Okay, maybe not so young. Someone that age should know better. "Don't worry I'll protect you from her." Charlie patted him on the knee.

"He just might need it," Lauren added with a half laugh. "Her behavior on New Year's Eve was obsessive."

***

The wedding rehearsal began promptly at four-thirty. Charlie got the impression that everything around here started and ended exactly on time. She found this strangely comforting. She liked things to happen when they were supposed to. It just made life simpler. More organized.

From her seat on the lawn she watched as the wedding planner explained what each member of the wedding party needed to do. Though she'd never been in a wedding, she didn't really see any great need for a rehearsal beforehand. The chances of anyone there not having been to a wedding before or at least seeing one on TV were slim, so unless the bride and groom had something unusual planned, a rehearsal seemed like a waste of time. Even if it seemed pointless to her, it did give Charlie another chance to observe Jake with his family. Not to mention it gave her a chance to enjoy her surroundings. With its well-manicured gardens, sprawling lawns and view of the ocean the property around Cliff House was just as magnificent as the mansion itself.

Despite the breathtaking scenery, Charlie didn't find herself focusing on that. Instead her eyes zeroed in on the interaction between each of Jake's family members. The camaraderie between Jake and his half-brother Dylan and between Jake and Callie spoke volumes. At the same time Charlie could sense tension between Sara, Jake's full sister, and everyone else. Especially between Sara and Callie.

What is the deal between them? While everyone else appeared relaxed and bantered back and forth, Sara remained rigid and spoke only when someone drew her into the conversation. Perhaps she'd ask Jake; assuming they got some time alone together. So far it hadn't happened. They'd been surrounded by people since getting there, though Jake promised they would get plenty of time to themselves before the weekend ended.

Charlie hoped he was right. She'd made the trip with him for that very reason even though she knew her time would be better spent back in North Salem. Not only could she provide help to anyone who needed an extra hand, but she could be mulling over her own decisions without Jake around as a distraction. She'd hoped getting away from Norfolk for a while would help her make up her mind about her career in the Navy. Yet she'd been in North Salem for weeks now and she was still up in the air on whether to stay in the Navy or return to civilian life.

True she still had time. The final decision didn't have to be made this month, but she wanted to decide soon. Leaving things up in the air drove her crazy. The sooner she made up her mind the better. If she chose to leave the Navy, she opened herself up to a whole new world of decisions and opportunities. If she stayed, life would proceed pretty much as it had for the last several years. So the big question was did she want to enter uncharted territory or stay with the safe and familiar.

Every decision she'd made in life so far gravitated toward safe options. Even when it came to men and relationships she picked the safe options. She dated only men who wouldn't capture her heart and then walk out once they did. At least she always did until now. Somehow she knew Jake could do some serious damage to her heart if she let him. They'd only known each other a short time and already she felt more emotionally connected to him than any other man she'd dated. How had she let that happen?

He's not looking for long-term either. Jake's the kind of guy who hangs around for a while then moves on when he gets bored. There's nothing to worry about. Except my heart.

Charlie forced herself to recall some of the magazine headlines she'd read over the years about Jake. They always painted him as the handsome playboy with women across the globe. Even though her mind pulled up plenty of names and incidents connected with his, Charlie wondered if it was all true. A month ago she would've said yes, but not now. Some of it had to be true. Pictures didn't lie, yet a picture could paint a misleading story.

From the altar Jake winked at her and Charlie's heart skipped a beat, something she'd never experienced before. Without a second thought she smiled and waved back, not once considering what his family would think if they saw her. She assumed they were already wondering what kind of relationship existed between them anyway. After all one didn't normally invite a virtual stranger to a family wedding. At least in her world people didn't. Yet if they were curious no one said anything to her.

***

"I've thought about this all day." Jake wrapped his arms around her waist and pulled her against him now that they were finally alone.

Charlie melted against him enjoying the warmth of his solid chest on her back and Jake's possessive embrace. Around them the crickets sang as the waves crashed against the shore. Above them stars sparkled liked diamonds in the clear sky.

Now this is romantic. A night to remember. She suspected she could live out the rest of her life and not experience a more romantic setting.

"Sorry we didn't get much time together earlier." As he spoke Jake nuzzled the side of her neck. "Sunday it'll be just you and me. Promise."

He whispered the last part of his sentence in her ear, filling her with desire that unfolded in her belly then spread like fire through her body. Words never affected her this way. They never made her want to throw her arms around a guy and beg him to make love to her. Beg him to make promises that he wouldn't be able to keep. Yet Jake's words were doing just that. More than anything she wanted to turn around and tell him to take her to his room where they could both enjoy the magnetism between them.

So what if she did? They were both adults. Who would care? Nobody.

"Family comes first." Charlie struggled to form a complete thought despite the sensations coursing through her body as he began to kiss the other side of her neck. "And this is your sister's wedding. I shouldn't even be here."

Jake's arms left her waist and he spun her around so she faced him. "Did Sara say something to you?"

His initial reaction took her aback. Had his sister complained about his choice of dates? The youngest

Sherbrooke hadn't joined the rest of the family until the wedding rehearsal, so Charlie had barely spoken to her. Still, she had noticed that Sara kept herself somewhat separated from everyone during both the rehearsal and the dinner party that followed.

"We only talked for a few minutes. She just asked how we met. Why, do you think she said something?" Charlie found it odd that he'd suspected Sara and not anyone else.

Jake took a deep breath and slowly exhaled. "Sara doesn't trust people much anymore thanks to her last boyfriend. Not even family. When she met Callie last year she was less than accepting. Even now things are a little rocky between them."

"Oh," Charlie said, now starting to understand why Sara had kept to herself during the rehearsal. "Really no one said anything. But most people don't take virtual strangers to family weddings." She might as well tell him exactly what she thought.

Jake's stance relaxed and he once again wrapped his arms around her. "What better way to learn more about each other than to spend the weekend together."

Talk about not getting the point. Did he really think bringing her along was no big deal? Perhaps he did things like this all the time. "Do you always invite strangers to your parents' house?" The question slipped out before she could stop it. "Forget I even asked. It doesn't matter," Charlie said disgusted by her lack of control. She didn't have a monopoly on him.

Jake chuckled and she felt his chest rumble beneath her breasts.

"You're the first I've invited to spend the weekend."

A warm tingly feeling spread through her body at his words, and Charlie fought it down. She didn't for one second want to think she was special to this man. She didn't want to think that he viewed her any differently than he did any other woman he spent time with.

"And it's not like I just pulled you off the street."

Charlie couldn't argue with him there. They'd seen each other every day since his arrival in North Salem. Still, she knew he didn't get what she meant, but she didn't feel like pressing the issue either. Why ruin the mood?

"I'm probably going to leave Massachusetts either Tuesday or Wednesday. There isn't much else that I can do there and I've got issues waiting for me in Virginia."

Jake's words brought an unexpected and unwanted physical pang to her heart. She knew his departure was inevitable. She had in fact been expecting it. Despite this, sadness rolled over her.

"How much longer will you be up here? If it's going to be awhile I can come back up but otherwise I thought we could see each other when you get back home." Jake looked her in the eye as he spoke.

His question sent her mind into overdrive. He wanted to continue their relationship or whatever this was past his time in North Salem. But did she? Could she continue to spend time with him and keep her heart firmly locked away? She'd never doubted it with other men but with Jake the uncertainty plagued her. Perhaps if she could figure out what it was about him that reached her on such a deep level, she could adequately protect herself. As of yet she hadn't been able to narrow it down.

"Not sure. I have a few more weeks of leave. I plan on spending at least some of it up here." She hadn't decided when she would go back to Virginia. Charlie found being with her family a nice change despite the hurricane and the destruction it caused. Not to mention that on this trip she felt no urgency to return home. On her last visit up she'd counted the days till she could get back in her car and drive home.

In the bright moonlight she saw Jake nod his head.

"I'll plan on coming back up then. Maybe next weekend."

Before Charlie could say anything, Jake grazed her lips with his. The kiss started out gentle, but quickly it changed as he applied more pressure. Soon he set about coaxing her lips apart, and Charlie happily gave him access. At the same time he slipped his hands under the hem of her shirt. Slowly he ran his hand up her back leaving a trail of fire across her skin. Unwilling to do much of anything else Charlie circled her arms around his neck and enjoyed the fire coursing through her body. Right then under the moonlight outside a nineteenth century mansion with the sound of the waves in the background and the fragrant smell of flowers around her, Charlie felt like the heroine from a classic black and white movie.

Jake took his time getting to know the contours of her back and Charlie relished every second of it. Once his hands made it to her shoulders, he let them begin to wander down her back. When they reached the hooks at the back of her bra they slowly circled around to the bottom of her rib cage. Charlie inhaled deeply as his fingers skimmed over her ribs before cupping her breasts. At the same time he kicked up the intensity of his kiss sending white hot desire spiraling through her body. Then inch by agonizing inch he pushed her bra down till his hands were on skin. She'd been with men before, but she'd never felt passion like this. Charlie feared her legs might give out so, unable to do much of anything else, she tightened her hold on him as he moved his lips away from hers and began to suckle the frantic pulse in her neck.

She moaned as his hand brushed across her nipple and she heard him chuckle. Part of her wanted to whack him for laughing but another just wanted to stand there forever while he lavished her body with attention.

In the end Charlie decided on a third option, to return the sweet torture. So she pulled his shirt out of his waist band, slipped her hands under his shirt and mimicked the same trip he'd taken. She made it up to his shoulders when hushed voices brought her game to an abrupt end. Without warning, Charlie jerked away from Jake's embrace.

At first Jake looked about to protest. He actually took a

step toward her, but then he stopped.

"Damn. Who the hell is that?" He kept his voice low as he stuffed the back of his shirt into his pants.

Charlie struggled as she attempted to fix her own clothing. Talk about rotten luck. Whoever was out walking could have gone anywhere on the property and they had to head in this direction.

By the time she finished adjusting her top, she could clearly make out Dylan and Callie's faces. They walked holding hands and leaning into each other. Both looked happy and very much in love.

What would it be like to be in love with someone like that? The thought leaped into Charlie's head. The concept of love, marriage and happily ever after had never entered her mind, not even when she saw her friends getting married. But tonight the ideas were swirling around in her head.

"I didn't know you two were out here." Dylan stopped alongside Jake. "Hope we're not interrupting anything."

Charlie didn't miss the knowing look that Dylan gave his half-brother. Immediately her face flooded with heat. It could be worse. This could be his father, she thought.

"It's a nice night. They probably wanted some fresh air. Just like us. All the guests are making the house stuffy," Callie offered.

Charlie threw Callie a grateful smile for her efforts. "I didn't think a rehearsal dinner party was such a big deal." She guessed more than twenty couples filled the mansion and most were not part of the wedding party itself.

"In the real world they're not; in Warren's world it's another story. Most of them will be leaving soon I think. At least till tomorrow."

Charlie could hear the strain in Callie's voice. Evidently Dylan heard it as well because he wrapped an arm around her shoulder and pulled her close.

"Forget about them. Tomorrow at this time we'll be on our way to France."

During their earlier conversation Callie had told her all about their honeymoon plans. They planned to spend three weeks in Europe, starting in France. The entire trip sounded romantic. She'd seen some of Europe but never on vacation, it'd always been while on duty. Someday she wanted to return. Charlie especially wanted to see Ireland and Scotland where many of her ancestors came from.

"Rub it in, why don't you." Jake tossed back at his brother. "While you two are off sightseeing some of us have real work to do."

Dylan laughed a deep rich sound that Charlie found contagious and she couldn't stop herself from smiling as well.

"If you're trying to make me feel guilty little brother, it's not going to work." Dylan stopped laughing and gave his brother a knowing look. "Besides, you'll get your chance."

Jake shrugged at his brother's comment but remained silent.

Charlie expected Dylan and Callie to say goodnight and continue on, but instead Dylan turned his attention toward her.

"Jake said your family runs a bed and breakfast. How long have they done that?" Dylan asked.

Charlie met his intense gaze and nodded. "For a few years now. Before that my mom rented out rooms mostly to college students from Salem State. My brother convinced her to try the bed and breakfast route. So far it's working well for them."

"Renting to regular boarders seems easier," Dylan said, his attention still centered on her.

"Maybe. I never asked. And they don't complain." Charlie shifted her weight but kept constant eye contact.

"Steadier income potential if you're renting to college students as well. There are always down times for a bed and breakfast regardless of its location."

Does he always think in terms of dollars and cents,

Charlie wondered? "I don't ask them about their finances. But The Victorian Rose seems to be doing well."

"That's a perfect name for a bed and breakfast," Callie chimed in. "We'll have to check it out sometime."

Charlie saw Callie nudge Dylan in the side and she suspected it was some kind of hint to change the subject. Whether it had been or not, Dylan's next question wasn't related to her family or their business.

"I understand you're in the Navy. How do you like it?"

"Originally I just saw it as a way to pay for college. Now, I consider it my way of giving back."

Although Dylan might just be making polite conversation, she still felt as if he was interrogating her.

"Enough with the questions. Weren't you two going for a walk?" Jake asked.

"Do you think he's trying to tell us something, Dylan?" Callie asked grinning.

Dylan glanced in her direction one last time then turned his attention to his fiancée. "You might be right. See you tomorrow, Charlie. Jake I'll meet you downstairs in about forty minutes."

Charlie remained silent as they walked back up toward the house glad that Dylan and Callie decided to continue their walk.

"You're lucky to have such a good relationship with your family." She hoped he didn't hear the twinge of jealousy in her voice. She'd never seen such closeness between family members before. Even prior to her parents' divorce, her family hadn't been this close.

Jake held open one of the side doors leading into an empty hallway. "When they're not driving me nuts, I agree. What about you? You seem to get along well with your mother and brother." Jake held her hand as he led her down a deserted hall.

Opened myself up for that one. "Not like you. This is the first time I've visited them in almost a year. My mom and brother are tight, but I've been a third wheel since ..."

Charlie paused. How much did she want to reveal? Her relationship with her family began to change the day her father walked out on them. She didn't share that with many people. "… my parent's divorce."

"How old were you?"

"The divorce was official a few days after my thirteenth birthday. It came as a complete surprise when they separated the year before. A lot of my friends' parents were divorced but I never thought mine would be."

He squeezed her hand as an unexpected emotion squeezed her heart.

"Most kids probably think like that. Do you see your father often?"

Did she see him often? She hadn't seen or heard from him since the day he walked out and as far as she knew neither had Sean. She didn't even know if the man was still alive. "He didn't bother to keep in contact," Charlie said as they stopped in front of her bedroom door. She could hear the bitterness in her voice, but could do nothing about it. Her father's rejection shouldn't bother her, especially after all this time, but it still did.

Releasing her hand, Jake wrapped his arms around her. "His loss," he whispered inches from her mouth before moving in to kiss her.

The kiss was tender but still sent shivers of excitement to every nerve ending in her body. Soon the excitement from his kiss and touch washed away the bad memories of her childhood.

"Maybe we should go inside," Charlie suggested as he moved his lips away from hers and settled on her neck. If he continued to tease her like this, she wouldn't be held responsible for her actions.

Jake lifted his head just enough to answer. "I'd like nothing more, but …"

Charlie groaned at the sound of the word but.

"I promised to take Dylan out for drinks tonight. I missed his bachelor party because of the hurricane so this is my chance to make it up to him. We leave in less than an hour so that doesn't leave me much time, and I don't want to be rushed."

Rather than cool her passion, his words further ignited it. How much effort would it take to change his mind? Sneaking her hands under the hem of his shirt, she decided to see for herself. "Is that so?" She trailed her hands up his back toward his shoulders. "Are you sure I can't change your mind?" she asked her voice low.

She felt his lips curve into a smile against her neck.

"You wouldn't even need to try, but this time I need to go." He pulled back and dropped a final kiss on her lips. "But I promise to make it up to you tomorrow, Charlie."

The desire in his eyes matched the desire running rampant through her body, and she knew, if not for the wedding in the morning, he'd come in. Charlie let her hands fall back to her sides. "Go have your drinks then." She opened the bedroom door and took a step inside. "See you tomorrow."

After she closed the door she looked around the well-appointed room. What should she do for the next few hours? Although it was late she knew sleep wouldn't be coming anytime soon, thanks to Jake. The guy had some nerve to awaken her passion like that and then retreat.

A well-stocked bookcase stood in the corner of the room. Selecting a book about the history of nineteenth century Newport, Charlie settled outside on the balcony. Hopefully a little reading would get her in the mood for bed.

CHAPTER 7

The musicians on the balcony overlooking the outdoor dance floor launched into a slow ballad. Without warning Jake tugged her onto the dance floor where the bride and groom were moving as one to the music. Dinner had ended more than an hour before but many people remained seated, lost in conversation. Given the diverse guests present, Charlie assumed those conversations ranged from politics to fashion and just about everything in between. None of it mattered to Charlie though as she melted against Jake who wrapped his arms around her and moved her across the dance floor. She'd been looking forward to this moment all day.

"You look beautiful today," he whispered, his breath tickling her ear. "Do you know what I've thought about all day?" His voice took on a husky tone.

Charlie didn't respond, though she thought she could guess.

"Taking you some place private and losing this sexy dress of yours."

The blue of his eyes darkened with desire and an unexpected bout of self-consciousness rolled over her. Never in her adult life had she been self-conscious. Yet surrounded by all these beautiful people, it kicked in. Jake Sherbrooke, world-renowned playboy, dated beautiful women all the time and the thought of him seeing her naked suddenly worried her.

"What do you think?" He ran his tongue along the outline of her ear. "No one will miss us if we go now."

What did she think? She could barely put two words together when their bodies touched. Even the briefest of touches caused her thoughts to float away. Talk about annoying. She never lost her head over a guy. She'd always teased her friends for doing just that. Evidently it was true, what goes around comes around.

Pull yourself together. He's talking about sex, not flying to the moon, she reminded herself. "I say what are we waiting for?" Charlie tried to project as much confidence in her answer as possible. The last thing she wanted was for him to pick up on how unlike herself she felt tonight.

At some point during their dance one of his hands had come to rest on her ass, and now he gave her a gentle squeeze and reached for her arm that was wrapped around him. No one paid any attention to them as they weaved between dancing couples. Once free of the dance floor, Jake picked up his pace. Charlie wished he'd stop long enough for her to remove her heels. She didn't wear them often and they kept sinking into the lawn making it difficult to keep up.

Like the night before, Jake took her in through a side door that led into a hallway near the back of the mansion. "We'll use the back stairway."

Raw energy and excitement rolled off Jake in waves as they walked down the deserted hall, adding to her building excitement. The trip up the stairs was quick and at the top he reached for her and pulled her against him. As he kissed her she could feel his arousal through their clothes. Charlie could feel the pent-up urgency in his kiss as he teased her mouth open and thrust his tongue inside. Just knowing she caused his arousal sent a jolt of power to her brain. Never in her wildest dreams would she have imagined she could stir such desire in man like Jake Sherbrooke.

Somehow, without letting her go, they stumbled down the hallway. With one arm still wrapped around her, he used his other to open the door.

Charlie heard a distinct click and knew he'd locked the bedroom door behind them. This is it, she thought. She'd dreamed about this moment since their first kiss outside the hospital and now it was about to happen.

Jake let go of her long enough to pull off his jacket and vest. As he did, Charlie took the opportunity to look around at what she guessed was his room. Slightly larger than her guest room, it was distinctly masculine including the huge four-poster bed positioned opposite the bank of windows. A black and red Persian rug covered much of the hardwood floor and a tall chest of drawers sat between two other doors in the room.

Later she would have to check out the view from the windows. She suspected it was even better than the one from her room. Right now though she had another view she wanted to see. Turning on her heel, she noticed that Jake had pulled his white dress shirt out of his pants. Before he could begin to unbutton it, she moved closer to him and brushed his fingers away from the tiny buttons.

"Let me," she whispered against his lips. She heard a deep intake of breath and couldn't contain her smile.

Charlie took her time undoing each tiny pearl button. Between each one she placed a gentle kiss on his lips or caressed his arm or back. The change in his breathing let her know her actions excited him. As she trailed a hand down his chest she wondered just how long she could tease him before he turned the tables. Jake didn't give her the opportunity to do anything else before tearing his arms out of the shirt as soon as she slipped the final button from its hole. The white t-shirt he wore underneath immediately followed, both of them quickly landing in a pile on the floor.

Jake with clothes on was gorgeous, but half-naked he was simply a sight to behold. Unable to stop herself, she ran a hand over his powerful chest then down his sculptured abs. She felt his abs contract and a new feeling of empowerment flowed through her. Without pausing she let her hand travel down further toward his belt buckle. With deliberate movements she undid the buckle making sure her hand brushed over his erection more than once.

After her third pass, he gripped her wrists. "I suggest you let me finish." Jake didn't wait for a reply. Once he undid his tux pants and added them to the growing pile on the floor he took a step back toward her. "My turn."

He began by pulling the pins from her hair. Once the twist she'd fashioned was gone, he slid his hands over her bare shoulders and back to the zipper of her dress. Inch by agonizing inch Charlie felt the zipper move downward until the only thing holding the dress up was the fact that her body was pressed tightly against Jake.

"I think it's time we get rid of this." As Jake whispered in her ear he took a step back and the dress began to fall away from her body.

Determined to remain calm, she fought the unexpected urge to grab the dress and yank it back into place, and when the dress hit the floor around her ankles she deliberately stepped out of it. Her heart pounded an erratic rhythm as she stood there in nothing but her white lace thong, strapless bra and heels. Despite her discomfort she never once looked away from Jake's face.

The raw desire she saw on his face as his gaze slowly and seductively slid down her body extinguished any fears and replaced them with a burning desire that set every inch of her body on fire. Her entire body craved his touch and she wanted nothing more than to fall into the bed behind them, wrap her body around his and satisfy her craving. With every intention of doing just that Charlie took a step toward him, but Jake reached for her first and held her in place. Slowly his eyes traveled from her face down to her feet and then back again. As his gaze moved over her it left a trail of pulsing excitement behind on her skin.

"You're sexier then I imagined."

Whether because of his compliment or the way his eyes devoured her, Charlie's confidence grew stronger. Before she could rethink her decision, she undid the tiny hooks at the back of her bra and tossed it on the floor. At the sound of Jake's sharp intake of breath she smiled. Before she could do or say anything else he closed the gap between them and scooped her off her feet.

The hard muscles of his chest and arms felt warm and secure against her already overheated skin. What would it be like to be held like this every day? To wake up in the morning surrounded by his arms and to fall asleep every night tucked safely up against his chest? Charlie couldn't dwell on the questions for long because Jake's mouth once again settled possessively on hers and thoughts of anything but the feeling of his warm hard body against hers disappeared into the night like smoke blowing in the wind.

Without breaking contact with her mouth, he deposited her in the center of his bed. Then with excruciating slowness Jake made love to her mouth with his lips and tongue while he teased and caressed the rest of her body. Though she wanted to reciprocate the sweet torture, he wouldn't allow it. Every time she tried to reach for him, he pushed her hands away.

"This isn't fair." Charlie moaned as she tugged at his thick hair.

"Seems fair to me," Jake whispered, his breath warm against her nipple.

She wanted to argue but the sensations coursing through her body were too exquisite.

Jake seemed to take his time learning every inch of her body. By the time he was done kissing and caressing her, Charlie was close to begging him to take her. Then just when she opened her mouth to beg him to end his torture, she heard the rustling of a foil package.

***

The heavy fog of sleep slowly dissipated and Jake opened his eyes. Right away he was aware of two things. The early morning rays of sunlight were streaming through his window and Charlie's warm body was pressed up against his. Sliding a hand under his head Jake replayed the events of the night over in his head, and a smile immediately spread across his face. Sex with Charlie had been everything he'd expected and more.

From the moment he led her off the dance floor she was an active and eager participant in their lovemaking. She teased him almost to the breaking point when she undressed him. It was as if he was a teenager experiencing sex for the first time. He stopped her when he did because he was afraid he would embarrass himself by coming the second their bodies joined. Yet when he reversed the tables and undressed her, it didn't help much. He knew she'd be sexy as hell naked, but still he wasn't prepared for the sight of her standing before him in a lace thong and bra. The woman was a mix of surprises. On the outside she presented herself as a strong Navy officer who always had everything under control. Every once in a while, however, he caught a glimpse of sadness in her, like when she spoke of her family. And her choice of underwear showed that despite her usual style of dress she definitely had a feminine side.

Next to him he felt Charlie move and he looked over at her. The sun coming through the windows danced across her bare skin making her red hair glow like fire against the black silk pillowcase. Instantly he felt something in his chest relax and a complete sense of peacefulness settled upon him. Often disappointment and the urge to keep searching plagued him. Neither emotion had bothered him for some time. In fact he hadn't felt either since kissing Charlie for the first time outside the hospital. He didn't know what that meant. However, he did know that he wanted to explore this thing between them. She seemed open to the idea. If she wasn't would she have made the trip this weekend with him? Would they have made love three times during the night?

As Jake continued to study Charlie and think about the way she made him feel, her eyelids began to flutter. Slowly her eyes opened and stared up at him. He could tell it took her a minute to fully realize where she was and he knew the second it dawned on her.

Charlie sat bolt upright in bed and tugged the sheet against her chest. Jake almost laughed at her attempt to cover herself. The night before he'd seen and explored every inch of her naked body. It seemed a little late for modesty now.

"What time is it?" she asked.

His fingers itched to pull down the sheet she clutched against her chest and pick up where they'd left off earlier, but he resisted the urge. She didn't appear to be in the right frame of mind at the moment so instead he glanced at his watch. "Six," he answered as he pulled himself into a sitting position next to her.

Charlie groaned and moved to get out of bed. "I shouldn't be here. If I wait too long your mom or someone else might see me going back to my room."

Jake shrugged. He didn't see why that should matter. "I doubt it, but so what? We're all adults."

"Your mom wouldn't even let Dylan and Callie share a room." Charlie threw him a look that would probably stop most people in their tracks. It didn't faze him though. Actually he found it cute and couldn't help but say so.

"You're adorable when you do that." He reached for her before she could comment and pulled her under him, silencing any retort with a kiss.

At first Charlie held herself stiff with her hands still clutching the sheet and her lips pressed tightly together. After a little coaxing she relaxed under him, and her arms looped around his shoulders.

"Don't go. Stay a little longer." Jake trailed a hand

down her side to her waist. He felt her quick intake of breath. *She's going to stay.* A sense of pure male satisfaction surged through him.

Charlie shook her head. "Can't. I don't want anyone to know I spent the night here." Disappointment laced her words.

"My family probably assumes we're sleeping together anyway. It's not like they think I'm a monk." The words passed his lips and he knew it'd been the wrong thing to say.

Nice going. Next to him Charlie eyed him. Without even asking he imagined Charlie was envisioning every headline and every picture of him ever printed. Time for some damage control, he thought.

"Come on Charlie. I'm twenty-eight. They know I'm not a virgin. The media has made sure of that."

She didn't get out of bed, but she didn't make any move to continue their earlier activities either. Instead Charlie continued to study his face as if looking for some hidden answer. "I know that." Her voice was confident but soft.

Once again he found himself cursing the media and the false picture it painted of him. Sure he dated, but the playboy they made him out to be didn't exist. In truth it never had.

"Really don't worry about my mom. She wouldn't say anything to you even if she did see you leaving my room. She'd come to me."

Charlie narrowed her eyes at him, and he suspected that she was deciding whether or not she believed him. After what seemed like an eternity, she relaxed next to him.

"I still don't want anyone to see me going back to my room." Leaning over, she kissed him on the cheek. "I'll see you downstairs at breakfast."

He decided not to force the issue. More than anything he wanted her to be comfortable this weekend. If being seen leaving his room would embarrass her, it was best to avoid it. If possible anyway. Even if she left now there was no guarantee she'd make it back to her room without someone seeing her in the same dress as the night before.

Jake didn't point this fact out to her. Instead he remained silent, content to watch her get dressed. Unlike many of the women he dated, she wasn't stick thin. She looked toned and healthy with curves in all the right places. He could stay here all day and look at her.

"How about we spend some time on the water today then head downtown for dinner?" Jake folded his arms behind his head and leaned against the headboard. He figured a day on his sailboat would give them some privacy from the members of his family who planned to stay in Newport for the week. So far, except for the hours they'd spent in his room, they hadn't gotten much alone time and tomorrow they were headed back to Massachusetts.

Charlie zipped up her dress then checked her reflection in the mirror. "Sounds good." After running her fingers through her hair she turned toward the bedroom door. "See you in a little while."

An unexpected twinge of disappointment shot through Jake's chest and he couldn't stop himself from getting out of bed to stop her. "What no goodbye kiss?" He tried to keep his voice teasing as he reached for her.

"Thought I already gave you one," Charlie answered stepping into his embrace.

Jake didn't argue. Rather he set about giving her a kiss designed to make her regret her decision to leave.

***

"So what do you do when you're not rebuilding towns after a disaster?" Charlie asked as they walked down Deblois Street later that afternoon.

Jake heard the gentle teasing underlying her words and decided to play along. "Mostly chase women in my fast cars. You'd be surprised how fast a woman wearing a pair of Prada heels can run."

Charlie laughed. It was a rich full laugh and Jake thought it suited her perfectly. A laugh like that couldn't be faked. It was genuine, just like everything else about her. Perhaps that was what drew him to her. There didn't seem to be anything false or contrived about Charlie. What you saw was what you got.

"I wouldn't know. They don't exactly go with my uniform and I doubt they would be comfortable for doing my rounds." Charlie stopped in front of an art gallery window where several paintings sat on display. Though each depicted a different landscape they all captured life in New England during one of its four distinct seasons.

"Seriously what kinds of things do you work on when you're not out in the field?"

She didn't look at him when she asked the question. Rather she seemed focused on one particular painting in the window which featured a family of four on a picnic. From the city painted in the background there was no mistaking it as a park somewhere in Boston. Although a nice painting, Jake didn't see what made it so interesting to her.

"Administrative business. Fundraising. Follow up on projects. The budget." Jake turned away from the glass window, more interested in looking at her rather than the art on display. "Do you want to go in and look around? You seem really interested in that painting."

Charlie's shoulders slumped ever so slightly and she frowned. "I've never been on a picnic."

He could hear the deep sadness in her voice. A sadness that seemed too intense to be caused by the mere detail she'd shared with him.

"I've eaten outside but I've never been on a real picnic like that one." She nodded toward the painting.

Jake opened his mouth to say something, but then closed it, unsure how to respond. Her slumped shoulders and mournful voice told him something buried deep down caused her sorrow. Something that had nothing to do with picnics, but he didn't know what or how to broach the topic. He was still trying to figure it out when Charlie turned to face him. Although the frown no longer marred her face, he could see the deep sadness lurking in her hazel eyes. Eyes that appeared almost green today thanks to her green top.

"Come on. Let's keep walking," she said as she took a step forward.

In silence they fell into step next to each other as they continued up the crowded downtown street. More than anything he wanted to banish the sadness he saw in her eyes. Prior to their stop she'd been laughing and relaxed. The woman walking with him now was quiet and solemn, not at all like the Charlie he'd come to know. Somehow he needed to lighten the atmosphere.

"How about we skip dinner and go for ice cream instead? Pirate's Cove is open. Nobody has better ice cream and we can play a round of mini-golf while we're there." It seemed like a feeble attempt even to him, but it was better than nothing.

When Charlie didn't answer he added, "Unless you're afraid you'll lose." In the short time he'd known her he'd learned she was not only headstrong and independent, but competitive. If anything would get her going it was a taunt.

Her reaction to his words didn't disappoint. Charlie's shoulders went back and the spark returned to her eyes. "You're on Mr. Sherbrooke."

They walked the couple of blocks to Pirate's Cove in silence.

"When you said ice cream and mini-golf, I expected one of those little outside stands with a tiny course," Charlie said as they joined the long line of customers waiting to place orders. The place they'd walked to was anything but tiny. A large eighteenth-century stone building with a flashing neon open sign sat way back from the road. To the left of the building was an enormous eighteen-hole mini-golf course complete with a windmill and waterfall. Behind the building were six batting cages and off to the far right was a go-cart track.

"You grew up in New England and never heard of Pirate's Cove?" he asked feigning astonishment. "You should be ashamed." The line moved forward and he moved with the crowd. "I used to come here all the time in the summer. They expanded the golf course and added go-carts a few years ago. I think they put in more batting cages too."

"Really? You came here in the summer?" Charlie gestured toward their surroundings her eyebrows raised.

"And that's supposed to mean what?" Jake knew the joking tone had left his voice and Charlie's slight blush told him she'd noticed.

Jake watched Charlie's shoulder's raise and lower. "Nothing. It's just that you could hang out anywhere in the world and this place seems ordinary. That's all."

Why did everyone think he considered ordinary below him? "There's nothing ordinary about their ice cream. They make it themselves." He tried to keep the irritation from creeping into his voice. Jake thought he'd accomplished this but Charlie's next comment told him otherwise.

"I didn't mean to insult you, Jake."

She dropped a feather-light kiss on his cheek and something in his chest tightened with emotion.

"Forget I said it, okay?"

"Said what?" he asked as they reached a window to place their orders.

CHAPTER 8

The following Wednesday night Jake called Charlie's cell while he relaxed in his entertainment room. When she didn't answer he left a short message and then checked his own three voice mails. The first was from his mother, the second from his sister Sara and the last one was from an old college buddy. He didn't plan on calling any of them back tonight. He already knew what his mother wanted. She wanted once again to broach the subject of him running for the state Senate. She saw it as a perfect place to launch his political career. A career he never planned on having despite his parents' wishes. He guessed Sara had called to just talk. She often did that, but he wasn't up for a long brother-sister conversation tonight. As for the call from Christopher, Jake guessed the guy was in town and wanted to get together. Normally when Christopher came to Virginia they'd catch a ball game or hit a few nightclubs. Neither activity held any interest to him tonight.

After grabbing the remote for the TV he flipped through the stations searching for something to distract him. The restlessness that plagued him when he wasn't in the field had returned as soon as he entered his office Tuesday afternoon. So far that week numerous pressing issues regarding the foundation had kept him busy but it wasn't enough. As usual he longed to get back into the field. Being cooped up in the office gave him too much time to dwell on his regrets; all the other things he felt were better kept locked away.

Tossing the remote onto the leather sofa, Jake abruptly came to his feet. The need to be moving was suddenly too great to ignore. What he wouldn't give for an excuse to get back into the field and to do some hands-on work. Or to see Charlie again. It'd only been two days, yet it felt much longer. He missed her more than he ever would've imagined considering the amount of time they'd known each other. He'd been in relationships before and been forced to spend time apart but it hadn't ever bothered him all that much. In the past he went on about his life, content to see the girls he dated whenever it was convenient for both of them.

This time the separation only added to his internal unease, an unease he hadn't felt in weeks. In fact he hadn't felt it since he'd learned of the broken dam and the destruction it caused in North Salem and headed to Massachusetts.

He'd expected it to return the minute he saw his parents at his sister's wedding. Oddly though it hadn't, at least not to the extent it usually did. Sure, he'd been frustrated by his father's grilling and his mother's hounding him about entering politics. Yet the normal feelings of regret and frustration at the fact that they couldn't accept the decisions he made hadn't presented themselves with Charlie around.

Leaving the television on, he opened the sliding glass door and stepped outside onto the deck. Splashes of pink and red painted the evening sky as the sun started to set, and a warm breeze stirred the air. Only one thing kept the evening from being perfect. He was alone. Not that he couldn't find someone to share it with him if he so desired, but he didn't want just any woman. The one he wanted was hundreds of miles away.

What was she doing tonight? Had she gone out for an evening run? He knew that she liked running at night. When he'd asked her about it, she told him it helped her to relax after a stressful day. Had she decided to head out for a run tonight? Or was she busy helping her mom in the kitchen? When he'd left there had been a few displaced citizens still staying at the Victorian Rose. Either way he couldn't do anything about it. Jake dropped down into a chair and stretched his legs out in front of him. Then he forced his mind to focus on the meeting he had first thing in the morning.

Jake remained outside until the stars filled the sky. Inside he could hear a sportscaster talking about the Orioles starting lineup for their game against the Rangers. He pushed himself up from the chair intending to go in and do some more channel surfing. He received every channel under the sun. There had to be something worth watching on one of them. His ringing cell stopped him in his tracks. It was Sara's ring tone. Since he knew she would only keep calling until she finally got him, he pulled the phone from his pocket and answered.

"Have you seen this week's copy of Today magazine?" she asked after greeting him.

He'd been expecting her to ask how he was, so when she asked her question he was momentarily thrown.

Dread settled in his chest making it feel as if an elephant had just sat on him. He knew his lawyer had called Marcy Blake to convince her to back off the story. She'd told him she would think about it. By the sound of his sister's voice, the reporter had made her decision. Damn. He couldn't wait for Blair to get the paternity test done so he could put this emerging scandal behind him. But Blair and her lawyer were dragging their feet.

"No. It's not on my reading list." Jake rubbed at the tension building in his neck. "I'm guessing you have, so tell me. How bad is it?" He tried to keep the aggravation out of his voice. His sister hadn't caused the situation so there was no need to take it out on her.

Sara didn't reply right away, and he took that as a bad sign. "Out with it, Sara."

"It says you walked out on Blair Peters when you found out she was pregnant a few weeks ago."

Anger and frustration washed over him. Jake slammed his fist down on the deck railing but he didn't get the satisfaction he desired. What he wanted was to physically destroy something. His preferred object of choice was Marcy Blake's computer, but at the moment just about anything would suffice.

"It also says you're already seeing a new woman."

Had someone at the wedding decided to capitalize on the fact he'd attended the wedding with a guest? Or was the reporter once again making up stories? Jake walked back into the house. The semi-tranquility he'd found outside had disappeared the minute Sara told him about the magazine headline.

"I thought you should know," Sara said softly with real concern in her voice.

"Thanks. I have an appointment with my lawyer again tomorrow. I guess we'll have to step up the pressure to get the test done." Jake clenched his fists as he fought to keep his emotions wrapped up.

On the other end of the line Sara cleared her throat. "Is there anything I can do to help? Maybe if I talk to Blair I can..."

"Thanks for the offer but I don't want you talking to her, Sara. For now I think the best thing to do is let the lawyers handle things." Knowing that Sara as well as Dylan and Callie believed him about Blair helped alleviate the annoyance he felt toward his parents who doubted him. However, he didn't see how Sara confronting Blair would help the situation. In fact, it might only make it worse. Blair was after revenge or money or maybe both and a little girl talk wasn't going to change her mind.

"Okay, but if you change your mind let me know." Sara paused before continuing. "Are you still seeing Charlie? Have you told her about this situation? She deserves to know, if you haven't."

Jake almost dropped the phone. No he hadn't mentioned it to Charlie because he'd hoped his lawyer would take care of the problem so he wouldn't have to. If it was on the cover of Today magazine though, Charlie may have already learned about it.

"Damn!"

"I'll take that as a no."

"Sara, I've got to go but if anyone asks you about this-"

Sara didn't give him a chance to finish his sentence. "I have no comment. Come on Jake I know the drill."

"I know you do. Listen, thanks for the heads up."

"Call me if you need to talk or anything."

Surprised by Sara's comment, he didn't respond right away. Lately he was the one to offer help not the other way around. "Okay."

After ending the call with his younger sister Jake dialed Charlie's cell again. If she hadn't seen the magazine cover yet, he wanted to explain things to her before she did. While he'd rather tell her in person, he also didn't want to wait till he saw her Friday night. And if she had seen the article he needed to do some damage control. Something that also couldn't wait till Friday.

Like before, Charlie's phone rang several times before kicking over to her voice mail. Again he left a short message only this time he told her he needed to talk to her about something important. Then he hit end on his phone and sent it sailing across the room in frustration. The brand new smart phone hit the wall and then the hardwood floor with a thud.

***

The traffic light turned red and Charlie brought the car to a stop. Grocery shopping was not how she wanted to spend her evening. Yet she'd promised she would do it while her mom went to the doctor's office. Her mom had felt lousy all week, but that afternoon she'd come down with a high fever. She'd only agreed to see the doctor after Charlie promised to get the groceries.

When the light turned green she turned left down Maple Street and noticed that things looked even better today than they had the day before. In fact it seemed like every day things in town got a little closer to normal. Last week most of the town had still been without electricity but today everyone had power. The majority of the fallen trees and other random pieces of debris had been removed so that the streets were again accessible. It seemed almost impossible that only weeks before a hurricane had swept through knocking out the dam and turning the town upside down. Sure, work still remained, especially on the dam and the homes that had been flooded, but for the most part people were now able to go about their everyday lives again. Even the schools were open again.

Most of it wouldn't have happened if not for Jake and his foundation. At the thought of him her heart rate increased and her body quivered in anticipation. He was due back in town on Friday and she couldn't wait to pick up right where they'd left off Monday night. On his last night in town they'd stayed up late exploring every inch of each other's bodies before falling asleep wrapped around each other. Not wanting her mother to know how she'd spent the evening, she woke up before dawn on Tuesday morning and returned to her own bedroom. If her mom or brother suspected anything sexual existed between them neither said anything to her. The only indication her mom gave that she suspected something was a brief questioning look when Charlie told her Jake was returning and would need a room. She'd used the excuse that his return was to check on progress but she didn't know if her mom believed her or not.

Not that it mattered. She didn't have to explain her actions to her family. If she chose to be involved with Jake it was her business and hers alone. It didn't concern anyone. Besides, she didn't plan on marrying the guy. They were just having some fun together. There wasn't anything wrong with that. They were both consenting adults, free to be with whomever they wished. Even now he might be with someone. The words "committed relationship" had never been spoken. Neither of them had expressed the desire to be solely with each other.

Before she could stop it from happening, a vision of Jake with his arms wrapped around another woman popped into her head. Anger and jealousy doused the previous anticipation she'd felt. Charlie gripped the steering wheel until her knuckles turned white and tried to purge the image from her mind, but it stubbornly stayed. The traffic light ahead turned red and she brought the car to a stop.

Pull yourself together, she thought. What did it matter what he did on his own time? They weren't in an actual committed relationship. There were no emotions involved. Theirs was a strictly physical relationship.

"The type I prefer," Charlie said as a reminder to herself. Once you let emotions enter the arena, relationships become too dangerous. They leave you exposed. Physical ones are safer and easier to control.

When the light turned green, she hit the accelerator while repeating her thoughts over in her head. Yet the jealousy remained, churning in her stomach and making her wish she'd skipped lunch.

Gradually her jealousy dissipated and by the time she walked into the supermarket, she had her emotions back under control. The green-eyed monster was defeated.

With a shopping cart full of groceries, Charlie headed to the front of the store eager to check out.

The magazine rack at the checkout was loaded with the usual tabloid magazines as well as copies of Time and National Geographic. She had no interest in the tabloids. Charlie knew that magazines like them would print anything to increase sales even if it meant making up stories. How else could you justify how two magazines could report completely opposite stories about the same people at the same time. So as she stood in line she didn't even glance at the tabloids, instead she reached for the most recent edition of National Geographic. Charlie opened the cover prepared to flip through the pages when another cover caught her eye. Behind the magazine she'd picked up sat a copy of Today.

Jake's intense blue eyes stared back at her from the magazine's cover. It wasn't the first time she'd seen his picture on a magazine cover and she knew it wouldn't be the last. Unable to stop herself, Charlie reached for the magazine, her curiosity too great to do anything else. Instantly she wished she hadn't. The headline below his picture read, *Prince Charming, Jake Sherbrooke soon to be a father.* The words sent her heart plummeting to her feet. Charlie stared at them. Maybe if she looked long enough they would change or disappear altogether. They didn't.

"Do you plan on buying that?" the young cashier at the registered asked as she snapped her chewing gum.

The young woman's annoyed tone pulled Charlie back to reality. Without a second thought, she handed the magazine to the cashier.

Once outside she tossed the bags of groceries into the trunk as fast as humanly possible. Then she climbed in the front seat and pulled open the magazine. Colored pictures of Jake with a dark-haired woman who looked almost too beautiful to be real greeted her. Below the pictures was an article by Marcy Blake, the reporter Jake had told her about.

Charlie clenched her teeth as she read the words. Was it true? Had Jake walked out on his pregnant girlfriend, Blair Peters? According to the article he had. Dropping the magazine onto her lap she took a deep breath. She didn't want to believe it about him. But it was possible. He did have the reputation of being a playboy. Yet the Jake she'd come to know didn't fit with his reputation. That combined with the way he acted around his family made it hard to believe he could walk away from an unborn child.

You've only known him a few weeks. A person could pretend to be anyone for that short of a time.

Charlie raked her fingers through her hair then picked up the magazine to reread the article. Unfortunately a second pass didn't change its contents. Unease clawed at her. Was Jake just like her father? A man willing to walk out on his children without a backward glance? Even an unborn child?

As if on autopilot she slid the key into the ignition and started the car. Just as she was about to shift into reverse her cell phone rang. She recognized the number on the display. Jake. He'd called her the day before and promised to call her sometime today.

Charlie picked up the phone and held it with her thumb poised over the talk button. Did she want to talk to him right now? She wasn't sure. Hell if what the magazine article said was true she didn't ever want to talk to him again. Avoiding him wouldn't answer her questions though. Still that didn't mean she had to speak with him now. Later after she digested the article might be a better time to question him.

After a few more rings the phone became silent, and Charlie tossed it onto the passenger seat. Then after one more glance at the magazine on the passenger seat under the phone, she headed back to the Victorian Rose.

CHAPTER 9

Jake drummed his fingers on the steering wheel Friday night and waited for the car in front of him to move. Traffic on I-95 hadn't budged in five minutes which only added to his current state of frustration.

Thanks to a combination of bad luck and a hectic schedule, he and Charlie had played phone tag on Thursday. Or at least he told himself that was why they hadn't spoken. His subconscious kept telling him a different story. While she had returned two of his calls and left messages when he didn't answer, she had not gone out of her way to reach him. Did that mean she was avoiding him? Had she already learned about the situation with Blair?

The uncertainty had been making him edgy all day. Earlier he'd nearly snapped Cindy's head off when she'd asked if he'd finished some reports. He'd immediately apologized, but he still felt like a complete ass. She didn't deserve to receive the brunt of his temper.

When he pulled into the parking lot of the bed and breakfast an hour later the outside lights welcomed him. Jake carefully maneuvered his rental car in between a Prius and Charlie's Jeep then killed the engine. For a moment he considered leaving his bag in the car. If Charlie had seen the magazine article she might tell him to get lost. Even if she hadn't seen it, once he explained the situation she might decide being involved with him wasn't worth the headache and show him to the door.

How much easier life would be if he hadn't been born a Sherbrooke. Once again Jake found himself envying his half-sister Callie who had grown up not knowing the truth about her father. In so many ways she'd had a better life than him, though he'd never admit that to anyone. If he did, it would make him look like a complete ass. People saw all the privilege and opportunities he had. They didn't see the paparazzi who shadowed him just waiting for a juicy story. Or the people who used their association with him only to satisfy their own agendas.

Get off the pity train. Jake climbed out of the car and started to close his door. At the last minute he pulled it open again and grabbed his bag from the back seat.

The sweet smell of fresh apple pie greeted him when he walked in. Immediately his mouth watered. He had breakfast but meetings kept him busy through lunch and his dinner on the plane had been less than satisfying.

Closing the door behind him, Jake looked around. The dining room to his left as well as the sitting room to his right were empty, but he could hear voices coming from the back of the house. He decided to head in that direction when Maureen O'Brien walked down the hall toward him wearing her flowered apron.

"Jake, it's nice to see you again. Charlie said you were coming up this weekend." Maureen gave him a motherly hug. "We just ate, but if you're hungry I can make you something." Her soft spoken voice and warm embrace instantly made him feel at home.

"It's good to see you too. If you have any leftovers that'll be fine."

Maureen started toward the kitchen and nodded for him to follow. "Follow me. Charlie's putting the leftovers away now."

Jake hesitated for a second. Charlie was his only reason for being here, and he hated not knowing what to expect from her. Would she throw him out the minute she saw him? Or would she give him a chance to explain. *Only one way to find out.*

Charlie stood at the counter covering plates of food with plastic wrap. From where he stood it looked like roast beef and roasted potatoes, and there was half an apple pie on the counter near the coffee pot. Immediately his mouth began to water. He'd always been a meat-and-potatoes kind of man. Fancy dishes that looked as if they belonged in a museum of modern art were fine on occasion but nothing could beat a good steak or roast.

"Sit down, Jake. I'll fix you a plate," Maureen said as she took a clean plate from the cupboard.

Jake stopped near the kitchen table but didn't pull out a chair. Instead he waited for Charlie to turn and acknowledge him. So far she hadn't even said hello. As the seconds ticked by his stomach clenched in dread. He opened his mouth to ask if he could speak with Charlie alone when she whipped around and took the plate from her mom.

"I'll do it. You've been busy all day, Ma. I can finish up in here." Charlie looked over in his direction for a brief second. With her face devoid of any emotion, there was no way for him to tell what thoughts were running through her mind

She didn't toss you out on your ass. It's a start.

Maureen didn't argue. Instead she removed her flowered apron then hung it up on the hook by the door. "Jake, I'll take your bag up on my way. I put you in the Hawthorne room again."

"Thank you." Jake waited until Maureen left before speaking again. "Hey." He kept his tone natural. He figured it was best to let her set the tone of the conversation. "How have you been?"

Charlie shrugged as she arranged several slices of meat on the plate. "Things around here are returning to normal. I think I'll head back to Virginia soon."

After heating the food in the microwave, she carried it to the table. "There's plenty more if you're still hungry after this."

Although the aromas drifting up from the plate had his caused his stomach to growl, he didn't reach for the food. Before he did anything he needed to explain things. "We need to talk." Charlie's less than enthusiastic greeting suggested she'd seen or heard about Blair. Still he didn't know for sure so Jake assumed the best place to start was the beginning. Pulling out a chair he gestured for her to have a seat.

Charlie didn't say anything. Rather she took a deep breath then slowly exhaled before sitting down. "Do you remember me mentioning a reporter named Marcy Blake?" Jake asked sitting down next to her. He wanted to reach for her but forced his hands to remain on the table.

She nodded yes but her face remained emotionless.

"She did an article on me in this week's edition of Today magazine." Jake wished she'd give some hint of her feelings.

"I know. I read it." He heard just the barest hint of anger in her voice. "They picked a great picture of you for the cover."

Okay, so she knows. Now the important question is, will she believe me? Jake leaned forward in his chair as he fought down his anger. The article had not painted him in a good light. "Blair and I dated for several months, but I ended things with her almost 3 months ago after I got back from a month in England."

Charlie folded her arms across her chest and her face went grim. "Is that when she told you she was pregnant?"

For a moment his temper flared. He knew the article claimed he walked out after she broke the news to him. "No. I only heard about it when I was up here. And it can't be true. If she's pregnant the baby isn't mine."

Next to him, the rigidness in her body relaxed but the guarded expression remained.

"The last time we slept together was more than four months ago. Wouldn't she have known before last week that she was pregnant?"

"Maybe. Maybe not. Everyone is different. Or she might have just waited to tell you."

By the cold tone of her voice, Jake knew she hadn't accepted his side of the story. Somehow though he needed to convince her. "Since you're the doctor I'm not going to argue about her knowing sooner. But we always used protection and if it is mine why won't she have the paternity test done? She won't even agree to an ultrasound to determine how far along she is." If he'd had any doubts about the baby being his, Blair's lack of cooperation proved to him that either she wasn't pregnant or she wasn't far enough along for it to be his.

Charlie's eyebrows came together in confusion. "I can understand her not wanting DNA tests done before the baby is born. There are some risks involved doing it prenatally. An ultrasound is harmless though." As she spoke she unfolded her arms and rested her hands on the table just inches away from his hands.

"Our lawyers have talked multiple times. She refuses. Of course Marcy Blake didn't mention any of that in the article." Jake picked up his fork and stabbed a piece of meat wishing it was the reporter's head instead.

Jake ate as he waited for Charlie to respond. Even though he was anxious to know her thoughts, he didn't want to push her. Regardless of what he told her, it still came down to his word against the media. A dull ache formed around his heart. Maybe if they'd known each other longer she would be more willing to accept his side of the story.

After finishing half the meat on his plate, Jake turned his attention to the roasted potatoes. He had a forkful in his mouth when Charlie finally spoke.

"What are you going to do next?" Her voice sounded more normal. Much of the coldness he'd heard before was gone. "You could wait till the baby is born."

He swallowed the food and shrugged. "I don't know yet. My lawyer is looking into my options." Jake didn't want to discuss how he was going to handle this problem with Blair. Instead he wanted to know where he stood with her. Eventually everything with Blair would be settled even if it did take several months. But he needed to know if she believed him enough to stick around and learn the truth. "I'm meeting with him again next week."

Charlie fell silent again and Jake could almost see her brain processing everything as she studied him.

"Charlie I know you have no reason to believe me." He reached out, lacing her fingers with his. "But if I thought the baby could be mine, I'd try to smooth things over with Blair. I would want to be a part of my child's life. But I don't believe her. The timing is all wrong, and she's too uncooperative."

She wanted to believe him. Everything she'd learned about him so far told her that he wasn't the type of man who would abandon a child. Then again her mother had probably thought the same thing about her father. At the same time she couldn't help but think of the scandal from the previous year with Jake's half-sister Callie. Sure Warren Sherbrooke claimed Callie's mother never told him about the pregnancy. Who really knew the truth though? Callie's mom was dead. Had it been a similar situation? Was Jake merely following in his father's footsteps?

On the other hand all the evidence he'd given her did seem to support Jake's claim, and since their first meeting he hadn't given her any reason not to trust him.

Why would his ex lie about this though? Blair had to know the truth would come out at some point. There was no way it wouldn't.

"If you want me to leave just say the word." He released her hand and pushed his chair back. The sound of the chair legs scraping across the tile floor was the only sound in the room.

She caught the hurt in his voice and knew she'd caused it. So far she hadn't given him any indication of where she stood on the issue and she probably wasn't the only one doubting him right now.

You're having fun with him, not marrying him. If it turns out he's lying it's not your problem. Charlie reached for his hand and tried to block out the nagging voice in her head that kept telling her if it did turn out to be true she'd be devastated.

"No. I want you to stay."

He squeezed her fingers tightly. "You believe me?" There was a slight tinge of wonder in his voice.

Pushing aside the tiny inkling of doubt, she nodded. "You haven't given me any reason not to."

For the first time since arriving, a true smile spread across Jake's face and Charlie nearly forgot to breathe. He always looked handsome, but his smile had a magnetism all its own. It almost seemed unfair to the entire female population. Honestly, how could any woman resist him?

"I missed you. I couldn't wait to get up here this weekend to see you." As he spoke he caressed her palm with his thumb. The gentle touch sent shivers up her arm.

"Missed me or my mom's cooking? You seemed to enjoy that quite a bit when you were here last time." She couldn't help but tease him because it accomplished two things. One it lightened the atmosphere, and two it drew her attention away from the feelings his admission sparked in her. True, men she'd dated in the past had told her they missed her but the words had never made her feel all warm and tingly before. Jake's words did just that.

"Both, but maybe the cooking just a bit more." Jake answered with a trace of laughter in his voice.

She couldn't stop herself from laughing as she stood

and walked over to the counter where a half of a pie sat. "I should've known. Nobody can compete with Ma's pot roast and apple pie." Charlie sliced two pieces of pie and carried them over. "It's a good thing you haven't tried her pecan pie. She'd probably never get you to leave then."

"I wouldn't stick around for pecan. Never liked it. But if she makes pumpkin or blueberry, that's another story."

***

Charlie climbed out of bed the next morning before Jake awoke. Part of her wanted nothing more than to cuddle up next to him and go back to sleep herself, but at the same time she didn't want anyone to see her leaving his room. She suspected her mom and brother knew he'd come back to see her, but neither had outright asked her. After all, she had spent the weekend in Newport with him. Still that didn't mean she wanted either of them to see her coming out of his room. So after one more glance at Jake, she slipped out the door and headed up to her room.

When she walked into the kitchen two hours later showered and dressed, she expected to find her mom preparing breakfast. Instead she found her mom sitting across the table from a dark-haired woman dressed in a powder blue sheath dress and matching blazer. A basket of fresh blueberry muffins was in the middle of the table and a mug of coffee sat in front of each woman.

Instantly the hairs on the back of Charlie's neck went up. She didn't recognize the woman but the small notepad in front of her suggested that she was a reporter which meant her presence had something to do with Jake. Why else would a reporter be sitting in her mother's kitchen drinking coffee and eating muffins?

Hoping to alert Jake before he came through the door, Charlie turned to leave just as her mother looked over and saw her standing in the doorway.

"Good you're up. You should be able to help Ms. Blake since you've spent a lot of time with Jake. She's doing an article about The Falmouth Foundation for her magazine."

131

It took all of Charlie's control not to groan when she heard the name of the woman. "I can try. We worked together a lot right after the hurricane." Charlie didn't know for certain but she suspected the reporter's reason for being there had nothing to do with Jake's foundation. "The town wouldn't have started to recover so quickly without the Falmouth Foundation."

"I'm hoping to get some insight into Jake Sherbrooke the man, not just his organization. People know a lot about the Falmouth Foundation and all the good it does already. They're more interested in Jake himself. They want to know what makes a man like that tick."

As the reporter explained her purpose for doing the article she smiled. While Charlie assumed the smile was meant to make her feel comfortable, it had the opposite effect. The smile made Charlie feel like some kind of prey and the reporter was getting ready to move in for the kill.

I bet they do, Charlie thought as a surge of protectiveness swept through her. What people wanted was more gossip, something she had no intention of giving. "Sorry. I can't tell you much. I didn't get a chance to really know him. I can tell you he's a hard worker. He did whatever needed to be done. He even boarded up windows," Charlie said with just the right amount of regret in her voice. "Maybe you can talk to some other people in town."

Marcy Blake's smile changed ever so slightly and her eyes narrowed. "Your mom mentioned you went to Newport with him for his sister's wedding. You must have gotten to know him a little during that time."

Nice going Ma. One of these days her mother's willingness to talk to anyone was going to get her into trouble. Charlie couldn't think of a good reply to the reporter's statement. Denying she had gone wouldn't work. Not only would she be saying her mother lied, but it seemed probable that the reporter could confirm it on her own. "We spent most of our time with his family. Family seems very important to him."

As she tried to think of other general items she could use to satisfy the reporter, she listened for approaching footsteps. With every minute that went by it became more likely that Jake would walk in looking for breakfast. She knew the last person he'd want to see seated at the kitchen table was Marcy Blake.

"How serious are things between you and him?" Marcy asked turning to an empty page in her notepad.

Like I would ever tell you. "We're friends," Charlie answered, pleased at how nonchalant she sounded.

Across the table her mother waved a hand in the air dismissing Charlie's comment. "She doesn't believe me. I keep telling her he wouldn't have come up here this weekend if they were just friends. Don't you agree? Men don't drive that far more than once in a week to see friends."

Charlie envisioned herself stuffing the dish towel hanging from the stove in her mother's mouth. At this rate her mother was going to give the reporter enough information to write an entire book not just a single article.

"He's here now?"

Charlie could almost see the reporter's radar go up, and before she could reply her mom offered up an answer.

"He got here last night. I think he plans on staying till Monday. Right, Charlie?'

She wasn't positive but she thought she heard the reporter mutter 'interesting' as she scribbled something down on her pad. Her instincts told her she should ask the reporter to leave, but she held back. If she did, the nosy reporter would assume she was hiding something and that may only make things worse for Jake. So instead she poured herself a coffee and sat down at the table. If nothing else maybe she could run interference with some of the questions. Otherwise who knew what her mother might tell the reporter.

"So you're the woman that people saw him playing

mini-golf with in Newport." This time the reporter directed her question right at her.

Charlie found it unsettling to have people referring to her, yet it shouldn't shock her. After all she spent the weekend with a man that the media considered an international playboy. "We went for ice cream and decided to play a round." Charlie tried to keep her voice level and devoid of any emotion.

Marcy Blake scribbled something down on her notepad. "Has he told you how he feels about becoming a father?"

Charlie's knuckles turned white as she gripped her coffee mug. No matter what answer she gave it would come off sounding bad. "If he ever has kids someday, I'm sure he'll be a great father. Like I said he seems big into family."

"You mean when," Marcy replied raising one of her manicured eyebrows. "His ex-girlfriend Blair Peters is expecting. Didn't he tell you?"

Charlie pictured herself tossing the coffee mug at Marcy's head as she debated how to reply. Engaging in a pissing match with the woman would accomplish nothing, but she still couldn't resist the urge to defend Jake. "So she says. Now unless you have any questions about the work Mr. Sherbrooke did here, you should go. My mother and I have a lot to do this morning before the guests come down for breakfast."

Marcy Blake closed her notepad and stuffed it into her Coach bag. "Of course. I have some other stops to make before I leave town anyway." Marcy gave them both a blinding white smile. "Thank you both for your time."

Charlie released the death grip on her coffee mug and stood. "I'll show you out." She didn't trust the woman and wouldn't put it past her to wander around the house looking to talk to other guests or to run into Jake himself.

CHAPTER 10

Charlie felt Jake's arm drop across her shoulders and she willingly snuggled close to him as he pulled her against his side. At their feet sat the remains of their late afternoon snack.

"I didn't mean to drag you into this. But you need to be prepared for what might come next."

"Marcy Blake didn't get anything interesting from me. So relax." Though he seemed more relaxed now than he had when she'd told him about the reporter's visit, she could still feel the tension in his muscles.

"You don't understand. She's going to paint you as the other woman. It won't matter that we met after Blair and I split."

Charlie heard the anger and frustration in his voice, and she wondered who he was more upset with the reporter or himself. She sensed it was an even split.

"She'll put whatever twist she needs to sell more magazines."

Charlie pulled away from his embrace. The setting sun cast his face in shadows but she could still see his incredible sapphire blue eyes. Normally his eyes were bright with a devilish look, but this afternoon they were hard and filled with anger. "Let her. I don't care. If anyone asks me, I'll tell them the truth."

Jake gave her a pitying look as he shook his head. "You don't get it. People won't believe you." he said forcefully. "I'm not even sure my parents believe me. When they see whatever twist that vulture puts on this story, they'll probably doubt me even more."

Some of the anger left his voice only to be replaced by sadness. She understood the anger toward Marcy Blake and the media, but she didn't get his feelings toward his parents. When she met his family at the wedding they seemed close. "Why?" It wasn't any of her business, but she couldn't stop herself from asking anyway.

For a minute he looked away from her. She wanted to press him for an answer and had to bite down on her lip to keep quiet. When he turned back to her his mouth was tight and grim.

"You could say I've never been the dutiful son. They've always had this master plan for me and I've never followed it. Instead I've always gone out of my way to do my own thing. The one time they got their way is when they stopped me from joining the Navy, and I've regretted it ever since," Jake said.

Charlie kept silent as he began to explain. Somehow she knew he didn't share information this personal with everyone.

"They'd deny it but I think they wanted to turn me into a clone of Dylan. When I went to college I did everything possible to separate myself from him. Got into the club scene. Showed up with a different actress or model all the time. Hit the casinos in Vegas and Monaco. The media picked up on it and my reputation as a playboy was born."

She didn't want to believe him. It didn't fit with the man she knew.

Perhaps seeing the uneasiness on her face, he reached for her and pulled her close again. "I didn't sleep with all of the women I took to the clubs. I just created the image to show my parents I was my own man. But the media didn't know that. And my parents saw the pictures and made their own assumptions."

She could understand how everyone would come to that conclusion. Even she had believed that Jake was the playboy Prince Charming the media portrayed. His parents knew the real man, though, didn't they? She didn't think they would just blindly accept what the media printed about him. However, convincing Jake didn't seem likely. So instead of trying, she switched the topic back to his immediate concern.

"It still doesn't bother me. Trust me I can handle whatever she writes." Charlie leaned in and brushed her lips against his. A delightful shiver of desire ran through her at the brief contact and every inch of her body called out for his touch. Forcing herself to go slow she ran her hands up his forearms and over his well-defined biceps before making a path down his chest. As she moved her hands over his flat stomach she felt his muscles tighten. When she reached the hem of his polo shirt, she slipped her hands under and reversed her previous path. Under her fingers she felt his muscles bunch and tense. At the same time she heard the slight change in his breathing.

With her heart hammering in her ears she pushed Jake gently to the floor of the gazebo, their earlier conversation forgotten. As they kissed she felt his hand slip under her shirt and up her spine. His hands were callused from working outside but the roughness only seemed to intensify the experience of having his hands on her body again; an experience she didn't think she would ever tire of.

Through the thick haze of desire, she heard gravel crunching under tires. As if just awakening from a dream, Charlie remembered they were in the gazebo behind her mom's bed and breakfast. Not the best place for getting upclose and personal.

"Now might be a good time to go upstairs," Jake

whispered near her ear.

She could feel his uneven breathing on her cheek and she couldn't contain a smile. She liked knowing she could affect him just as much as he did her.

"Sounds like a plan to me."

Charlie tossed the remains of their snack into a basket. Later she would wrap the leftover blueberry turnovers. Right now her body urged her to work fast and get to a place where they could continue what they'd already started.

With everything cleaned up, Jake helped her to her feet and they sprinted toward the back door. She assumed whoever had arrived would go through the front entrance. Only family used the door that led into the kitchen. She guessed wrong though and almost collided with Sean.

Sean remained silent as he glanced from Charlie to Jake then to the basket. "Need seconds that badly?" he asked finally.

"Something like that," Charlie answered. She sensed her brother knew exactly where they'd been heading.

"Don't let me stop you." Without another word he walked back toward his loaded pickup truck in the driveway.

From here she couldn't tell what all the boxes in the truck contained, but she guessed it would take Sean awhile to carry them all inside by himself.

Next to her Jake let go of her hand. "Need help?" he called out as if reading her mind.

Turning around to face them again, Sean eyed Jake for a moment before answering. "If you're offering, I'm not saying no."

Her brain knew it was the right thing to do, and if Jake hadn't offered, Sean never would've asked. Still, disappointment washed over her. Removing boxes from her brother's truck was not what her body wanted to be doing right now. It wanted to be upstairs removing Jake's clothes instead.

"The bed isn't going anywhere," he whispered in her ear, his warm breath caressing her cheek. "Your brother and I can take care of this if you want to go in," he added before kissing her.

"Are you sure? I don't mind." The more people working the sooner she and Jake could continue what they started.

"Jake's right. We've got this. Go on in."

"Don't say I didn't offer." Charlie didn't have a good reason to argue with her brother so she carried the remains of their snack and went inside.

Jake watched her walk into the house then joined Sean at the back of his truck.

"Gonna be around long?" Sean asked.

"Till Monday." Jake pulled a large box out of the truck bed.

Sean reached for another as well but didn't pick it up. "Does Charlie know about your pregnant ex? If not I suggest you tell her."

Jake didn't miss the threatening tone of the statement. He wanted to hate the guy for it, but if the tables were reversed he could see himself doing the same thing. How many times had he done similar things on Sara's behalf? More times than he cared to count.

"I don't want her hurt. Understand? And your arm wouldn't be the first I've broken on my sister's behalf without her knowledge."

He didn't doubt Sean could do it without breaking a sweat either. Charlie's brother reminded him of a brick wall. "She knows everything O'Brien. Just for the record it's not mine."

"Glad to hear it," Sean said, his voice losing its menacing tone.

If whatever existed between him and Charlie was going to continue he didn't want any bad blood between him and her family. "Are we good then? Or is this going to be a problem?"

"We're good." Sean slapped him on the back before lifting his box and starting toward the house. "A reporter stopped at Quinn's Hardware asking questions about you," Sean said before disappearing down the stairs around the side of the house that led into the basement.

And today just keeps getting better. "Just me?" Jake wondered if Marcy Blake made that stop before or after her stop at the Victorian Rose.

Sean dropped the case he carried and motioned for Jake to do the same. "At least while I was there she only asked about you, but I left before she did. Why?"

Jake heard a trace of the threatening tone from before return to the other man's voice, and he wondered if Charlie realized just how protective her brother could be. He doubted it.

"She stopped here this morning," Jake said as he headed back outside.

"And Ma was a wealth of information," Sean said before Jake could comment any further.

"You could say that." Once again he felt guilty for dragging Charlie and her family into this new scandal.

"Leave it to her. She just doesn't know when to stop."

The need to defend Maureen O'Brien's behavior fueled Jake's next comment. "It's not her fault. Marcy Blake could get a corpse to talk. That's why she's so good at her job."

Sean stopped near his truck and leaned against the side. "Ma means well, but she likes to talk, always has. I hope she didn't say too much."

"Nothing that Marcy couldn't find out from some other source." Jake reached for another box. "But you should be prepared for other reporters if and when Marcy writes about Charlie coming to Newport with me."

Sean groaned and pushed away from the truck. "Great. Just what we need. More chaos around here." He pulled the next case off the tuck bed. "On second thought it might be good for business," he said after a minute. "After people read the President's son stayed here they might figure it's good enough for them too."

Sean walked toward the house. "Hey, maybe I should put a plaque outside the room you used. Billionaire playboy Jake Sherbrooke slept here. What do you think? Maybe I could charge a premium for that room."

Jake heard Sean laugh as he disappeared down the basement stairs. Guy's got a strange sense of humor, Jake thought following him down. "Always glad to be of service. Do you want me to sign it for you?"

"I like the way you think, Sherbrooke."

It took a few more trips to empty the truck but eventually all the boxes were stacked in the basement.

"You want a beer?" Sean asked closing the door to the storage room in the basement behind him.

He wanted to find Charlie and pick up where they'd left off in the gazebo, but sharing that information with her brother was out of the question. "Sounds good." Jake followed Sean to the opposite side of the basement.

"Do you play?" Sean asked as he opened the door to the refrigerator.

Since the pool table stood between them, Jake assumed Sean was referring to pool. "A little but not since college." He accepted the ice cold bottle Sean handed him.

"I don't play much anymore either. But before we started the bed and breakfast I used to play in a league. Now I get together with a couple of guys maybe once a month to play." Sean took a long swallow from his beer. "You up for a game?"

He doubted it would be much of a game. He'd never mastered pool, but in this instance that would be a plus since it meant the game would be over all that much sooner. Grabbing a pool stick off the wall, he approached the table. "Rack them up."

***

Much later that evening Jake laid in bed staring at the canopy above his head. He could feel Charlie's slow even breathing next to him as she slept, and he couldn't help but marvel at how right it felt to have her by his side. A part of him wanted to press a pause button and keep them just like this forever. He'd learned a long time ago how rapidly situations could deteriorate and loathed to see that happen between Charlie and him. He didn't know how far their relationship would go, but he wasn't in any rush to see it end. Something he knew could happen if the media threw their relationship into the spotlight. While Charlie insisted she could take anything the media tossed at her, he knew from experience that it could be far worse than she imagined it.

Although if anyone could handle it, he suspected it'd be Charlie. She wasn't one to take BS from anyone, and she didn't hold anything back. If Charlie felt a certain way she let you know it.

Even though he knew she could take care of herself, that didn't stop him from considering the different ways he might be able to protect her from unwanted media attention. He figured in the worst case scenario he could hire a private body guard to keep an eye on her. His family had done it in the past before his father took office and the Secret Service became a regular part of his family's life. They'd most recently done it when Callie's identity came out. If he did hire protection, Jake knew Charlie would hate it. Not that he would blame her. There was nothing fun about having someone follow you twenty-four seven. He shuddered at the memory of what it'd been like with the Secret Service following his every move. Thankfully the only time he interacted with them now was when he saw his father.

Jake rolled onto his side so he could look at Charlie and once again he marveled at the beauty sleeping next to him. Sure he'd been with beautiful women before, but Charlie's beauty was natural. It didn't need enhancing from makeup or fancy hairstyles. With his hand he brushed a few pieces of hair off her check and tucked them behind her ear. As if dead to the world she didn't stir as he let his fingers linger on her cheek. Part of him wanted to wake her, but he held back. Instead he climbed out of bed and tossed on a pair of shorts. He knew it'd be awhile before sleep returned so he pulled out his laptop and tackled his latest emails.

CHAPTER 11

"I've got good news and bad news," Jake told her over the phone one week later.

Charlie didn't like the sound of that. In her book nothing good ever resulted when someone began a conversation that way. "Give me the good news first." She cradled the phone against her ear as she continued to fold laundry.

"My lawyer got the ultrasound results from Blair's lawyer yesterday. Blair is 14 weeks pregnant. Her estimated conception date is in March. I was in England that entire month."

"Sounds like great news so what's the problem?"

"She could claim she was with me. Technically we were still together then. Or she could argue it's only an estimated date. The research I read said the technology is not one hundred percent accurate."

Charlie didn't see his bad news as earth-shattering. There must be people in England that could confirm Blair hadn't been with him. "No, but its pretty darn good. Besides whoever you were visiting can confirm you were alone right?" Although he'd left out any names, he'd told her that he recently visited family in England during one of their conversations.

Jake remained silent on the other end of the line and a knot began to grow in Charlie's stomach. What was he hiding? Had he left out some important details when he'd told her about his trip?

"I can't. I was visiting my cousin. He was in drug rehab. If I tell the media who I was with they'll start digging and AJ's hospital stay would come out. Right now no one but me and his girlfriend know about it. He doesn't want the rest of the family to know yet."

Charlie admired him for his sense of loyalty but didn't agree with his decision. If he could put an end to the speculation now, he should consider it. "Have you asked him?"

"Trust me, AJ can't handle it right now. I'll just have to wait it out. My lawyer is still pushing for DNA testing. Though her lawyer did suggest that she'd be willing to admit she might be mistaken in exchange for two million dollars. Apparently Blair is running a little low on funds."

How could someone blow through the money Blair Peters made modeling?. She modeled for all the top designers as well as Victoria's Secret. Charlie didn't know what the going rate for a fashion model was, but it had to be way up there.

"For that kind of money she should come right out and tell the truth."

"She wants to save face."

Charlie couldn't contain her sarcastic laugh. "So it looks better to admit she was involved with two men at the same time?"

"I guess it does in her mind. Not that it matters. I'm not paying her anything."

She still thought getting someone to verify his whereabouts during the month of March was the best solution. "Jake, maybe you should talk to your cousin. See what he says. He might surprise you."

"What are your plans for this weekend?"

Jake's immediate switch in topics let her know he considered their previous topic closed for further discussion.

Fool. She wanted to reach through the phone and beat

some sense into the man. "None, why?" she asked, choosing to take his hint and drop the subject.

"I thought we could spend it together."

A warm sense of excitement spread through her. It occurred every time she anticipated spending time with him. And she wasn't sure she liked it. None of the men she dated in the past affected her this way, and she couldn't help but wonder if that meant her feelings toward Jake were developing into something she didn't want to deal with. Every time they were together she tried to remind herself she wasn't looking for love. That she was only having fun with Jake. But somehow she suspected her heart was slowly getting invested in their relationship despite her efforts.

"What did you have in mind?" Charlie pushed aside worries for the moment. She could sort out her feeling later when they weren't on the phone.

"How does a weekend on Martha's Vineyard sound? I can pick you up and we can fly to the island together," Jake said.

The worries she'd just buried exploded in her head again. How should she interpret Jake and his actions? They never discussed an exclusive relationship, yet he treated it as one. He called almost every day. Sometimes they talked about nothing of importance. The weekend before he traveled up to see her and now he wanted to take her away. Just what was his game? Should she tell him she didn't want anything serious in her life? Or should she go with the flow and keep having fun? Eventually he would move on to someone else. She knew that like she knew the sun would rise tomorrow. So why worry about it now, right?

"It sounds nice. I've never been." Charlie proceeded to put her clothes away while ignoring the uneasy emotions lurking just below the surface. By agreeing to go was she leading him on and giving him the wrong impression about what she wanted? If on the off chance he wanted something permanent between them, he had a right to know the truth.

Get serious. This is Jake Sherbrooke aka Prince Charming. Even if he wanted a serious girlfriend he wouldn't look at you.

Though it hurt to admit, Charlie's silent reminder to herself pushed most of her unease away. Another relaxing weekend with Jake sounded wonderful, so why should she deny herself

"I'll take that as a yes," Jake drawled.

Charlie closed the bureau drawer causing her retirement papers to scatter across the floor. She'd been prepared to fax them the day before, and then had gotten distracted. For whatever reason she'd hadn't gotten around to it yet. "You twisted my arm. I'll go with you." She picked up the papers and put them back into their envelope.

"I knew I could convince you," Jake replied smugly. "I'll have a car pick you up and bring you to the airport. I'll meet you there."

***

Jake leaned back in the plush leather seat and stretched his legs out as his last conversation with his lawyer replayed in his head. He'd suggested that Jake consider paying Blair off. As much as he wanted this scandal to disappear, he refused to play her game. It now made sense why she repeatedly tried to change his mind about their relationship. She wasn't the first woman to use him for his money. Unfortunately, he didn't have another quick and easy way out of this situation. Not unless he wanted to drag his cousin into things. Charlie suggested he reconsider his decision on that front. He knew she meant well, but she didn't understand his cousin's fragile state. Even if he just announced that he'd been in England during March the media would somehow track down his exact whereabouts. They always seemed to. Once they did that, it wouldn't be hard to trace things back to AJ. He wouldn't let that happen. No one else in the family knew about AJ's problem and he'd promised to keep it that way. If it meant he had to make some sacrifices to keep his promise, oh well. Both his family and Charlie seemed willing to stick by him.

The fact his family remained behind him didn't surprise him. While they may not always agree or support his decisions, they would never turn their back on him. Charlie, on the other hand, did surprise him a little. The fact she had not tossed him out on his ass when she read the magazine pleased him, more than he thought possible in fact. After all, in many ways they barely knew each other. But at the same time he felt closer to her than any other women he'd dated. Jake didn't know what that meant in the long term, though he did know he was looking forward to another weekend together. This time away from both their families.

Reaching for his drink he realized this would be their first weekend alone. Every time they'd been together either her family or his were close by. The thought made him smile. No one else around meant no distractions or interruptions.

A few minutes later the small plane touched down. Eager to see Charlie, Jake came to his feet. If everything went as planned the car he'd sent to pick her up at the Victorian Rose would arrive soon.

A warm breeze washed over him as he stood outside the airport. A group of girl scouts passed him on their way inside for a tour of the airport, but Jake didn't notice them. His mind was planning the next few days. He already had scheduled reservations for dinner. But after that he had nothing planned. As far as he cared they could spend the entire weekend locked up in their room, coming out just for food. Still it wouldn't hurt to have a few other ideas just in case Charlie wanted to see some of the island. After all, it was her first time on Martha's Vineyard. Perhaps a short excursion for some sightseeing or shopping was needed. Many talented artists and jewelry makers called the island home.

The sound of several car doors slamming grabbed Jake's attention. From behind his dark glasses his eyes scanned the people heading his way. The minute his eyes locked on Charlie walking toward him a calmness he hadn't realized was missing settled over him. Until the moment he saw her, he hadn't realized how restless he'd been. With her suddenly in reach he felt grounded, as if he was just where he was meant to be.

He couldn't help but smile when she saw him and waved. Today her vibrant red hair hung free and the breeze was blowing it in every direction. She wore a pair of denim shorts and a plain black t-shirt. Although the outfit didn't scream "look at me", he couldn't tear his eyes from her.

"You're late," he said in his best no-nonsense tone. She'd told him before how much she hated being late so he couldn't help but give her a bit of a hard time now.

Charlie stopped in front of him, her hands on her slim hips. "Not all of us have a private plane, Mr. Sherbrooke."

She kept any hint of laughter out of her voice, but he noticed her lips curved ever so slightly as she fought back a smile.

"Some of us had to deal with traffic on the highway."

He stopped a grin from spreading across his face. She never held anything back. She seemed to tell him exactly what was on her mind. "I'll forgive you this time. Just don't let it happen again." Jake took two steps forward and pulled her possessively toward him. When his arms went around her it almost felt as if a switch flicked inside his head. The minute he felt her pressed up against him all of his worries faded away. That fact unnerved him. How could someone he'd known such a short time have such an effect on him? And what should he do about it?

Now isn't the time to think about it. This weekend is all about relaxing and having fun.

"The plane is waiting for us." Jake took a step back and picked up her bag. "Ready to go?"

Charlie took hold of his free hand and fell into step next to him. "All set."

Jake led her inside the airport and through a restricted area, then back outside to the private air strip where their plane sat ready to go. "I think you'll love the house we're staying in. It belongs to a good friend of mine. He bought it a few years ago, but only gets there maybe once a year." Jake put her bag in a storage compartment, then pulled her down into one of the seats and prepared to make this his most enjoyable plane ride ever.

***

Charlie walked along the uppermost deck with a mug of coffee in hand and took in the view. She couldn't imagine owning a piece of property like this and only getting here once a year. She didn't know where the homeowner spent most of his time, but it couldn't possibly compare to this. Setting her mug down on a table, she glanced over the railing at the secluded beach below. Maybe today she would check it out. Since it was part of the property no one else could use the beach, and it remained pristine thanks to the home's maintenance staff. She doubted even a single piece of drift wood could be found on the sand.

Through the open screen door she heard Jake moving around inside. When she woke up he'd looked so peaceful she didn't want to disturb him, so she'd made a pot of coffee and come outside. That had been more than an hour ago.

As she leaned against the railing she wondered what he had planned for the day. The previous afternoon they'd walked through the center of town checking out some of the local businesses before having a dinner at The Blue Herring, the most exclusive restaurant on the island.

He knows how to spoil a girl, Charlie thought as visions of their dinner replayed in her mind.

Behind her the screen door opened and closed. "Why didn't you wake me?" Jake wrapped an arm around her waist and pulled her against his side.

"You looked so adorable sleeping. I didn't have the heart," she teased before dropping a quick kiss on his cheek.

"Adorable? I looked adorable?" He asked with mock outrage. "I'm going to get you for that one."

"Just try."

Jake took a long drink of coffee before replying. "Those sound like fighting words."

"You can take them anyway you want," Charlie tossed back, enjoying the silly banter. "So what's on the agenda for today?" As she spoke Charlie looped her arm around his waist and leaned into his side.

"For starters, breakfast. It's ready when you are. After that you'll just have to wait and see."

After a breakfast of freshly baked scones and fruit, Charlie took her time getting ready. She felt no need to rush and Jake didn't seem in any hurry either. In fact, by the time Charlie showered and dressed the clock read noon and Jake still hadn't finished getting dressed

What are we up to today? Charlie sat in a leather recliner watching television while she waited for Jake. The slowpoke was still in the bedroom getting dressed. Whoever said women took forever to get ready obviously hadn't met a twenty-first century man.

She pressed the up arrow prepared to scroll through the TV stations a third time when Jake entered the media room. Water still clung to his hair making it appear a much darker shade of blond than usual. He wore shorts and a t-shirt indicating that his plans were casual.

"Let's go," he announced as he leaned one shoulder against the door frame. "Unless you'd rather stay inside."

Charlie switched off the television and stood. "I'm the one who's been waiting." She crossed to the door and stopped.

"I promise you won't be disappointed. But you do need

to wear this." Jake told her pulling a black bandana from his pocket and moving toward her.

Charlie pulled the bandana from his hand and held it over her breasts. "Well, if I'm going to wear this then you're definitely overdressed."

"Not a bad idea, but not what I had in mind," Jake said grabbing the bandana back and covering her eyes. Once secured, he took her hand.

Warmth spread up her arm and through her body at his touch as they walked down a set of stairs. He remained silent as he led her, and Charlie wondered just where he was taking her.

She could tell they were walking through the house though she had no idea in what direction. Soon she felt the ocean breeze on her face and she knew they were outside, most likely on the lower deck. In the distance she heard the roar of the waves, and the warm sun above beat down on her as Jake continued to lead her toward his surprise.

"Just one last step," Jake told her as he helped her down a staircase.

Charlie felt the surface beneath her sandals change from something solid to sandy and she knew they'd stepped onto the beach. They walked a short distance before Jake again stopped. "Okay, you can sit now."

A visit to the beach didn't seem like all that much of a surprise considering where they were, yet she didn't complain. After all it was a flawless day and she was on a private beach with possibly the most gorgeous man alive. Really what was there to complain about?

Sinking to her knees Charlie waited. Behind her she felt Jake loosen the knot in the bandana. When the cloth dropped she blinked a few times as her eyes grew accustomed to the bright sunshine. Then she really looked around. Spread out in front of her was a red and white checkered table cloth with a huge wicker basket in the middle. Two champagne flutes stood in front of the basket with a bottle of champagne on ice right next to them.

"Surprise!" he said dropping down to his knees next to her.

A picnic, she thought, unable to say anything around the lump in her throat. He'd brought her on an old-fashioned picnic. "You remembered," she whispered, her voice almost impossible to hear over the waves. "I can't believe you remembered."

Jake popped open the champagne bottle and poured her a glass. "Playboys have terrific memories. Didn't you know that?" he asked as he handed her a glass.

Charlie took a sip from her glass. The bubbles tickled her throat and she savored the taste. She generally preferred beer when she drank, but this champagne was the smoothest she'd ever tasted. "I didn't know that, but I'll keep it in mind for the future."

"If you ever have any other questions about us, don't hesitate to ask." Jake smiled at her as he began to pull food from the picnic basket.

Oh, she had questions all right. She just chose not to ask them. Some questions were better off not asked. "I'll remember that too," she promised accepting the dinner plate he held out.

All the food spread out in front of her looked good but she still held back. "It all looks great. I'm not sure what to try first."

Jake reached for a cherry tomato stuffed with what looked like fresh mozzarella cheese and basil. "I suggest you start with one of these. I stole one earlier and they're delicious." After placing it on her plate he reached for another. "I tried some of the focaccia too."

"Why am I not surprised?" Charlie popped the tomato in her mouth and chewed. Jake was right, it was delicious.

A better picnic never existed, at least Charlie believed so. Everything about their beach picnic, from the food to the location, was perfect. And the company wasn't half bad either, she thought looking over at Jake. Though she felt ready to burst from all the food she'd eaten, he sat munching on yet another brownie. Not that she blamed him. If she had any more room left she'd indulge in one more herself. Perhaps if any remained later she'd have one, although watching Jake eat, that possibility seemed unlikely.

Straightening her legs out, she leaned back and rested on her elbows. The hot beach sand warmed her bare legs and Charlie wiggled her toes underneath it. She almost never made it to the beach, but whenever she did she was reminded how much she liked it. Today even more so thanks to the company. Just being on the beach seemed to help wash away the stress of everyday life.

"You look deep in thought over there. How many pennies will it cost for them?" Jake's question signaled that he'd finished his most recent brownie.

"I'll consider this one on the house since you went to all this work," Charlie answered pointing to the remnants of their picnic. "I was thinking about how much I like the beach. I always seem to forget that till I get back to one."

"Then I'm glad I picked it for our picnic." Jake leaned over and dropped a kiss on her cheek. "I hope you enjoyed it."

Words didn't normally fail her. Actually she couldn't think of a time when she hadn't been able to express her opinion with ease. Right now, however, the right words escaped her. In silence Charlie watched the waves hit the beach and recede again. "I'll never forget it." The huge knot in her throat almost chocked off the last part of her sentence much to her frustration. She considered herself a calm cool woman, not someone ruled by emotions. This afternoon though she felt like just the opposite.

"Just want I wanted to hear."

She knew by his tone that he was smiling and turned to confirm her belief. Even though she expected it, the hundred-watt smile spreading across his face set her pulse racing. Damn, she should be used to that smile by now. What was wrong with her?

"You do know that no beach picnic is complete without a walk along the water?" Jake replaced the empty containers into the basket.

"Oh, really? So there are written rules for these types of things?"

Jake's eyebrow went up. "Of course. There's a whole rule book." His tone contained just the right amount of arrogance and playfulness. "And after a walk the couple must retreat to the nearest bedroom. It's all spelled out in the book."

She couldn't help but shake her head. Jake Sherbrooke made her laugh more than anyone else she knew. "Let's go then. I don't want to get caught breaking the rules."

Charlie let Jake help her to her feet and together they started down the beach along the shoreline. For a little while they walked in silence, but she didn't mind. In some ways she actually liked it. The lack of conversation let her focus on the sound of the crashing waves and the way the cool ocean breeze felt against her skin.

"Are you going to apply for that position at the hospital in Williamsburg?" Jake asked breaking the comfortable silence between them.

The week before, a former colleague who knew Charlie was considering retiring from the Navy had given her a heads-up about an opening at Memorial Hospital in Williamsburg, Virginia.

"I sent in all the paperwork yesterday. I don't know how long it will take to hear something."

Jake stopped walking and put his arm around her waist. "Does that mean you've decided to leave the Navy?"

The waves washed up over Charlie's feet as she stood staring out at the ocean. This was the first time he'd asked her if she'd made up her mind. Charlie wished she could say yes. But she couldn't. Actually she was no closer now to making a decision than she had been when she left Virginia. "Honestly I don't know yet. One minute leaving seems like the right decision and then the next I am telling myself it would be a huge mistake."

Charlie watched a boat off in the distance bob on the water and it reminded her of how she felt about her future. One minute she was optimistic about a change and then the next her enthusiasm plummeted. "Do you have any thoughts?"

When Jake didn't answer immediately, she turned to look at him and was surprised by the seriousness of his expression. His grin was gone and his eyebrows drew downward as if deep in thought.

"Unless you're sure you want to make the Navy your life, I think you should retire. This position in Williamsburg sounds like the perfect opportunity to move forward with your life without having to completely start over somewhere else. "

Charlie opened her mouth to respond but then closed it. Knowing how he felt about the military, she'd expected an entirely different answer from him. "I never thought of it that way," she said unable to come up with anything better.

***

Jake felt the wheels of the plane touch down but ignored it; content to sit kissing Charlie who sat on his lap with her arms wrapped around his neck.

Slowly he felt her pull her mouth away from his. "We landed," Charlie said, her voice echoing his own disappointment.

"So? We have a few more minutes." He settled his lips on top of hers again. A few more minutes weren't enough. What he wanted was another day with her. If he didn't have a meeting in Virginia tomorrow morning he'd ask her to stay in Boston with him for the night. Their two days together had flown by. In fact, she hadn't left yet and already he was thinking about when he'd be able to see her again.

Could he somehow reschedule his meeting for tomorrow? Jake ran through all that rescheduling would entail. The meeting was set for eight in the morning, so he knew it wouldn't give the other parties involved enough lead time.

"Next time we do this it has to be for more than two days," Jake said as they exited the plane. "And maybe to some place more exotic. Any thoughts?"

He wrapped his arm around her shoulders and entered the airport. As they walked he got the sense that they were being watched. Jake let his eyes wander in search of anyone unusual. At first glance he didn't detect anyone, but when he was about to shrug off the feeling of unease, he saw the photographer. He was trying to blend in with the other tourists, but he didn't quite fit in. He had no visible luggage and the camera hung around his neck was too high-end for an everyday vacationer.

"I hope you're ready for your magazine debut."

Charlie looked over at him, her forehead wrinkled in confusion.

"That guy in the black shirt and baseball hat is a photographer. I don't know for who, but I am positive of it." Jake knew it was only a matter of time before the media picked up on his most recent relationship, he just hoped Charlie was as ready as she thought.

"It might be a coincidence," Charlie offered.

Jake was glad to hear that she sounded calm about the whole thing.

"Maybe, but he saw us. He probably got a picture too." Any other woman he knew would be hoping the photographer had snapped a picture or two, not Charlie.

Charlie continued walking and didn't stop until they were standing by the car he'd arranged to take her home.

"He'll probably think about it later and decide it couldn't be you. Even if he did take a picture he'll think it must have been a look-alike. After all, why would *you* show up at the airport with some unknown redhead?" Charlie's tone told him she believed every word she spoke.

For the first time since meeting her, Jake associated her

with the word naive. If she thought the fact that she wasn't a celebrity would stop the media, she was in for a rude awakening. Perhaps if he'd shown up with an eighty-year-old man the photographer would second guess himself, but Charlie was a young beautiful woman, more beautiful than she seemed to realize.

"Don't count on it Charlie," he warned, dropping her bag to the ground and taking a step closer.

Charlie wrapped her arms around his shoulders and he felt her fingers dig into his hair. "I'm not worried about it."

Jake shook his head but didn't press the issue. "I'll call you tomorrow." Jake pulled Charlie tight against him relishing the way her body felt against his.

"Sounds good. Have a safe trip back."

He felt her fingers trailing up and down his neck. Once again Jake found himself contemplating if there was any way he could reschedule his morning meeting. "You too," he replied before lowering his head so he could kiss her. Though it took all of his self-control he kept the kiss short. "You'd better go now."

Jake waited until Charlie left and then went back inside to re-board the plane

CHAPTER 12

Charlie's cell rang for the third time in the past twenty minutes. A quick glance at the number told her what she'd already suspected. She didn't know the person calling and most likely didn't want to talk to them. Picking up the phone she set it to vibrate. Something she should have done yesterday when the calls first started. But honestly she hadn't thought the calls would still be coming in.

The first few had surprised her, although she supposed they shouldn't have. Jake tried to warn her about what would happen when the media learned about her. She'd thought he was exaggerating. Man, had she been wrong. Not only had reporters called her phone as well as the Victorian Rose's business line, but they'd descended on the bed and breakfast.

With the first few who showed up, she tried to be polite, but her patience wore out fast. By the early evening she'd stopped answering the door altogether. Instead Sean took over that duty. Sean could be intimidating thanks to his size alone, but Sean angry was something else entirely. And she knew for a fact that he'd threatened a few of the more insistent reporters.

Thankfully she hadn't heard the doorbell ring since that

morning. As much as she hoped that meant things were settling down, she doubted it. Rather she guessed the reporters were regrouping, just waiting for a better time to strike.

How long could their interest last anyway? Once they learned what little there was to know about her, they'd stop bothering her, right? The questions danced around in her head as she paced from one side of her bedroom to the other. Besides once she returned to Norfolk, it'd be more difficult for them to get to her. While her house wasn't on base, the hospital where she worked was. These reporters wouldn't venture onto a Naval base just to snap a few photos, would they?

When she'd put the question to Jake the night before, he'd told her that nothing was off limits when it came to the media. Then he'd offered to hire a private security guard for her. She'd immediately dismissed his offer, insisting that she could take care of herself.

Charlie crossed her room one more time and grabbed the book off her desk. For a moment she stared at the manila envelope containing her retirement documents. She'd finished filling them out weeks ago, but was now having second thoughts. Maybe tomorrow she'd sit down and really think about what she wanted.

After dismissing her professional future from her thoughts, she settled into the chair near the window. The night before, after talking to Jake, she started a classic Steven King novel and she hoped his master storytelling would distract her at least until Jake called. Their conversations always managed to keep her mind off whatever bothered her.

***

"Do you want to talk about it?" Maureen O'Brien asked when Charlie walked into the back flower garden Friday afternoon.

Charlie shoved her cell phone into her back pocket and shrugged. "Talk about what?" Without waiting for her mom to ask, she knelt down and yanked out a weed. Maybe if she played dumb her mom would leave her alone.

"Something is wrong. I can tell by your expression." Maureen stopped working and turned to look at Charlie. "And you've been edgy all day."

It was on the tip of her tongue to say everything was fine, but Charlie knew it wasn't. Ever since Jake failed to call her two nights in a row, she'd been on edge. Since he left North Salem, no more than a day had gone between his phone calls. The first day when his call hadn't come she'd chalked it up to his busy schedule. Then on the second day she received a short text that just said *can't talk tonight*. At the time she didn't question the message. Instead she assumed he would call her today.

For most of the day she fought the urge to call him herself. She didn't want to appear needy. But when four o'clock came and went, Charlie caved and tried his cell. It immediately sent her to voice mail.

"I expected a call and it never came." Charlie tore out another weed and tossed it on the wagon her mom used for gardening. "It's no big deal."

She spoke the truth. It just wasn't the whole truth. Right now though it was all she would admit aloud. If she acknowledged the sense of betrayal she felt lurking in the shadows, she would have to admit she had strong feelings for Jake. Something she wasn't sure she'd ever be ready to do.

Her mom didn't say anything, but Charlie could feel her mom's eyes on her. When she was a child her mom had always been able to see exactly what Charlie felt. After the divorce her mom became too focused on other things to really notice her anymore. Yet as Charlie sat there concentrating on yanking out weeds so that her mom could plant new flowers, she sensed for the first time in years her mom could see what was bothering her.

"Have you tried calling Jake?" Maureen asked as she moved closer to Charlie.

"Who said I was talking about him?" Charlie asked as she pulled out another weed with more force than needed.

Maureen wrapped an arm around Charlie's shoulders. "You didn't have to. I saw the way you looked at him when he was here."

She wanted to challenge her mom's statement, but it seemed pointless. Her mom could be almost as stubborn as her so changing her mind would be almost impossible.

"He didn't answer his phone." Charlie reached for another weed only to realize all the ones in that part of the garden were gone. "Just got a short text last night and nothing since."

Anxious to keep busy, Charlie moved away from her mom farther down the flower bed to a section her mother hadn't touched.

"What about his office? Did you try there?" Maureen asked as she gathered up her gardening tools and followed Charlie.

Charlie shook her head. "I'm not sure I should." The thought had entered her mind, but she quickly dismissed it. A call to his office might give the wrong impression. She wanted to keep this relationship or whatever it was between them light and casual. After all, serious entanglements were not her style; or his for that matter. A phone call to his office seemed like something a girlfriend would do.

"Bah." Maureen waved her hand in the air for extra emphasis. "Unless he said not to call, I don't see any harm in it.

Not once had he told her not to call the office. In fact the first time he returned to Virginia he gave her not only his cell number but also his work number. Still something held her back from using it.

"Why don't you go in and try him now. I can handle the weeding myself." Her mom gave her a gentle pat on the leg and proceeded to attack the weeds threatening what was left of her favorite rose bush. "You'll feel better if you do."

A nagging voice in her head kept telling Charlie that her mom was wrong. "It's late. The office is probably closed."

In the end Charlie waited another two hours before trying Jake again. Once again her call went straight to his voice mail.

Should she try his office? She tapped his business card against the desk in her room, uncertainty clawing at her. What was the worst that could happen? If he couldn't talk now, he'd tell her.

With her mind made up she punched in the number. After several rings someone answered. "Falmouth Foundation," a crisp female voice said.

Surprised that someone had answered, Charlie paused for a half-heartbeat before speaking. "I'm calling for Jake Sherbrooke," she said, her voice just as crisp and businesslike as the woman on the other end of the line.

"He isn't in the office."

Did that mean he wasn't in now or hadn't been in all day? "Do you know when he'll be back?"

"No. He flew out last night."

The simple reply made the already growing knot in Charlie's stomach double in size. "Is he away on business?" She didn't think the woman would answer but she asked anyway.

"I'm not at liberty to say. But if you want to leave a message you may. I expect he will be calling in at some point." The secretary remained businesslike, but Charlie thought she sounded a little less stuffy.

Leave a message? Saying what? "No that's okay. Thanks." Charlie didn't wait for a reply instead she hit the end button on her phone.

Unable to sit still, she walked to her window. The sky outside glittered with stars and a full moon dominated her view, however her mind was too preoccupied to really appreciate the view tonight. Where had he gone and why couldn't the secretary say. If he'd gone away on official business there wouldn't be any reason to keep his whereabouts a secret. She assumed that meant he'd left for a personal reason. And if that was the case why hadn't he told her? Why keep it a secret from her? Why sneak away?

Was that what he'd done? Sneaked away to be with someone else without the courtesy of telling her things between them were over first. Just like her father had done to her mother?

For the first time in years memories from the day she realized her father wasn't coming home flooded her mind. It'd been a complete shock to her when he left one morning and never came back. When he'd finally sent word a week later that he'd moved to Florida and wanted a divorce, the entire family had been devastated. Nothing was ever the same again.

A few tear drops trailed down Charlie's face as she fought to suppress the memories. Even if Jake had decided to call it quits without a single word she wasn't going to shed any tears over it. It wasn't as if she loved him or anything, she told herself. He'd just been another person passing through her life.

***

Charlie checked her emails then switched over to her normal web browser for any interesting world news. She brought up a story about a new space program initiative when her phone rang. When she checked the caller ID she expected to see Jake's number. Instead she saw her friend and temporary roommate Beth's number.

Beth was perhaps her oldest friend in Norfolk. They'd been transferred to the base a week apart and had both worked at the hospital on base. Beth lost everything when the apartment building she lived in burned down so she moved in with Charlie.

"Did you end things with Jake already? Are you crazy?" Beth asked after saying hello. "Do you know how many women would kill to be in your place?"

For a moment Charlie wondered why she told Beth about Jake in the first place. "If I'm crazy I'm not the only one. What are you talking about?"

For a full minute silence stretched out over the phone. "So you two are still a couple?" Beth asked slowly.

"You make it sound as if we're in high school," Charlie said exasperated. "We spend time together."

Dead silence again greeted Charlie's ear.

"If you're near a computer look at Today Magazine's site."

At the tone of Beth's voice ice began to form around her heart. Without asking anymore questions, Charlie typed in the internet address. Immediately a photo of some popular singer she'd never heard of popped up.

"When you have the site up, scroll down to the second article."

Charlie moved down to the second article and stared. The man in the photo looked remarkably like Jake and he had his arm around the shoulders of a petite blonde. Charlie forced her eyes away from the picture on the screen and read the headline above it. "Playboy Jake Sherbrooke arrives in London with yet another woman."

When Jake's secretary said he'd flown out, Charlie assumed she meant that he flew to somewhere in the United States not to another country. And although she didn't have any proof, she'd hoped that he'd only left Virginia for business, but the picture on the screen suggested otherwise. Did she want to read anymore, Charlie wondered as she moved the cursor toward the X in the right hand corner of the web browser? Part of her wanted to shut down the computer and ignore the picture on the screen. Unfortunately her jealous half refused to let her. She'd never been one to shy away from things no matter how difficult.

So instead of closing the link, Charlie read the short paragraph under the picture.

International playboy Jake Sherbrooke arrived today at

Heathrow International Airport. He was met by an unknown blond who greeted him with an affectionate hug. The couple then got into a black BMW and drove away. This rendezvous follows his most recent outing to Martha's Vineyard with a redhead who he reportedly took to his sister's wedding last month. And while Prince Charming dates beautiful woman on both sides of the pond, model Blair Peters is expecting his first child.

Below the paragraph there were two pictures. The first was a shot of Blair and Jake at some charity event back in January. The other photo was one of her and Jake at the airport in Boston when they'd returned from Martha's Vineyard.

She read the short caption a second time but the words didn't change. Without bothering to shut down the computer, Charlie slammed the laptop closed, then she pushed her chair back and came to her feet with so much force the wooden desk chair toppled to the floor.

"Are you okay?" Beth said, reminding Charlie that she was still on the line.

"Fine. Why wouldn't I be?" Charlie answered through clenched teeth. "We weren't in a committed relationship." As she spoke Charlie tried to keep her emotions from entering her voice.

"If you say so." Beth didn't sound convinced. "Charlie if you want to talk later or anything call, okay?"

With anger surging through every nerve in her body, Charlie paced between her bed and the window. "Don't worry. I'm fine. Thanks for calling. I'll talk to you soon."

After ending the call, she tossed the phone on her nightstand.

The two-timing jerk was off in England spending time with another woman. Did he expect her to sit around waiting for him to come back? Or did he think so little of her that he didn't feel it was necessary to tell her things were over? Either way she should've known better.

What else should she have expected from someone referred to as an 'international playboy'? And to think she'd believed his little story about how the media had it all wrong!

Grabbing a pillow off the bed, she punched it imagining it was Jake's face. He was probably lying about Blair and the baby too. More than likely the baby was his and he just wasn't man enough to own up to it. Evidently even billionaires could be deadbeat dads just like hers.

Damn! He really was no better than her father. How had she missed it? Had she been so overwhelmed by his good looks and average-Joe act that she hadn't seen the real him? She'd always considered herself a better judge of character than that. Obviously she wasn't. She was no better with men than her mother.

"That's not true. At least I didn't fall in love with him," Charlie said to herself. Yet somehow the words sounded untrue. If she didn't care about him, then his betrayal wouldn't hurt so much. True, she'd still be pissed but not hurt. "You're not hurt. These are tears of anger." Charlie wiped the few tears sliding down her face and struggled to keep any more from falling. "That snake isn't worth it." And if he ever called again she'd tell him what she really thought of him.

***

Charlie got the chance later that night when her cell phone rang. Without even looking she knew it was Jake. Did she want to answer and tell him to go to hell or just let it go to voice mail and not bother calling him back? Both options were appealing.

"Are you going to answer that?" her mother asked from across the kitchen.

Charlie pulled the phone out of her back jeans pocket and looked at the caller ID. Sure enough Jake's number filled the screen. "Be right back," she said as she marched out of the kitchen.

She waited till she was outside to answer. "Hello."

"Hey, how's my favorite doctor."

How could he tease her so affectionately when he'd

flown across the Atlantic to be with someone else? "Not interested in talking to you."

Silence filled the other end of the line and for a second she wondered if he was still there.

"You've got a strange sense of humor." Jake's voice took on a hesitant tone. "If you're mad because I didn't call sooner, I'm sorry. I've been busy and then there's the time difference."

"I know how busy you've been. I saw a picture of you and the pretty blond you're so busy with." A warm breeze blew around her and she could hear the crickets chirping in the grass creating a relaxing environment that was completely at odds with the anger raging inside of her.

"Blond?" Jake asked sounding truly confused. "Charlie I don't know what you're talking about. I'm in England. My cousin …"

"Don't bother feeding me any lines. I should've expected as much from someone like you." Maybe his lines worked with the other women he knew, but not her.

Once again there was silence. Part of her wanted him to deny her allegations, but she knew even if he did it wouldn't change anything. Pictures didn't lie and hadn't he already admitted he was in England just like the caption claimed.

Before he could say anything in his defense she added, "It's fine Jake. Really, I don't care. Enjoy your time in London." With her final sentence Charlie hit end on her phone and shoved it back into her pocket.

She should feel relieved. She told him what she thought without letting him know how much it bothered her. Yet all she felt as she walked back into the kitchen was shame and emptiness. Shame at herself for believing that Jake was different. For thinking that maybe he could truly care for her. And emptiness because she'd just lost a tiny part of her heart to him.

After the line went dead, Jake pulled the phone away

from his ear and stared at it. What the hell just happened? Yeah, he expected Charlie to be a little upset that he hadn't called sooner, but the conversation they'd just had made no sense at all.

Shaking his head he tried to replay the conversation over in his head. Despite his efforts it still didn't make any sense to him. Obviously she was upset about something. Should he call her back and try to straighten things out? Or would it be better to wait a little while, maybe give her a chance to cool down?

For some reason he doubted waiting would help the situation much so he hit redial. The phone range several times before going to voice mail. Even though he assumed she wouldn't call him back in her current mood, he left a message asking her to do just that.

Okay, you can figure this out. Jake paced in front of the empty fireplace. She'd referred to a picture of him and some blonde. He hadn't been out with anyone since meeting Charlie so what picture had she seen? Could it be an old one some magazine just released. Was some media outlet trying to play up the scandal already brewing with Blair? And why had she said he was in London? Had she guessed when he said he was in England? If she'd spoken to Cindy, she'd know he was in Bristol not London. He'd left a detailed message for Cindy to pass along if and when Charlie called. Was it possible she never got the message? But if she had spoken to Cindy she would know he wasn't here on some kind of vacation.

"AJ is out of the ICU and asking for you," Sophia, AJ's girlfriend, said walking into the room.

Lost in thought Jake hadn't heard her come in, but at the sound of her voice he stopped and turned. Petite and blonde, the two words echoed in his head. Sophia was both. Could Charlie have seen a picture of them together somehow? Sophia was the only woman he'd been around lately. Had a photographer taken a picture of them together and published it?

"Why are you looking at me like that?"

"Sorry. I have a lot on my mind. Listen I want to know how AJ is doing, but I need to check something out." Jake moved toward the guest room where he'd left his laptop. He didn't bother to wait for a reply. Instead he brought up his favorite search engine and typed in his own name. Several links came up, but he chose the one with the most recent date. After opening the link a color photo popped up and sure enough it featured him and Sophia at the airport together with a short article beneath.

"What are you looking at?" Sophia asked entering the room. "Is that us?" She peered over his shoulder.

"Bloody hell," he swore using one of Dylan's favorite expressions. "She must have seen this picture," he groaned running his hands through his hair. While he agreed the picture looked bad, he'd hoped that she had a little more faith in him. Didn't Charlie trust him at all?

"Who are you talking about?"

Jake turned away from the screen. He didn't need to see the picture or headline to figure out exactly what had happened. "Charlie. Someone I've been seeing. Just talked to her and she accused me of seeing someone else. That picture is why," he said gesturing toward the computer.

Damn it. Once again the media was butting into his life.

Sophia sat down on the edge of the bed. "If you explain, I'm sure she'll understand."

Without intending to Jake laughed sarcastically. "Would you? With my reputation to back up that photo?" Jake tried to ignore the dull pain settling in his chest. He'd really thought that Charlie had come to know the real him, rather than the Jake Sherbrooke the media liked to portray. Evidently, he'd been dead wrong. If she could jump to conclusions about him so quickly she didn't know him at all.

"Maybe. I'm not sure." Sophia shrugged.

Jake heard the uncertainty in her voice.

"You could at least try, Jake. It's her loss if she doesn't

believe you."

Sophia only had that half correct. If she didn't believe him, he'd be losing a lot too. During their time together he'd come to care about her in a way he'd never felt before. And he knew he would hurt like hell if she walked out of his life forever.

"How's AJ doing?" Jake didn't want to continue discussing Charlie. Later he'd try her again. He knew in her current mood, she wouldn't listen to him. Maybe if he gave her a change to calm down she'd hear him out.

CHAPTER 13

A week later Charlie sat on her bed packing. The following morning she was returning to Virginia. She had another week of leave left but she intended to spend it at her own place. She also had an interview at the hospital in Williamsburg. Although she'd hoped to make up her mind concerning her career in the Navy by now, she was still on the fence. Hopefully after this interview she would be able to make up her mind.

A mere week earlier, before she'd seen that picture of Jake on the internet, she'd been certain she wanted to retire from the Navy and start the next phase of her life. Now that he'd shown his true colors and she was back to thinking rationally, staying in the Navy seemed like an excellent idea.

But regardless of her ultimate decision, her stay in Massachusetts needed to end. Staying at the bed and breakfast surrounded by thoughts of Jake only clouded her mind. She needed to get back to a place where there were no memories of him.

Charlie grabbed the turquoise sarong from her pile of clothes and memories of her weekend on Martha's Vineyard came rushing back. She'd bought it while on the island, and it'd been sitting in the bottom of her drawer since coming back.

Rolling it into a ball, she stuffed the piece of fabric into her bag and wished she could roll up and discard her feelings for Jake just as easily. She'd been trying for the past seven days but so far she hadn't been successful. It was just a fun summer fling, she reminded herself. Something she could tell her friends about when she got back to Norfolk.

Charlie grabbed a t-shirt next and folded it before adding it to her bag. Why couldn't she forget about the jerk? Why the hell did he have to invade her thoughts all day? Hopefully getting home would help with that. At least he'd stopped calling her. His last call had been two days ago. She was surprised he'd called her back at all. Though she hadn't seen any more pictures of him and his unidentified blonde that didn't mean he wasn't still in England with her.

Man she'd been a complete idiot. She'd really believed everything he told her. Charlie couldn't remember ever being quite that gullible before.

She'd never let a man dupe her like that again.

Charlie pulled her second duffel bag onto the bed ready to fill it, when there was a knock at the door. "Come on in," she called as she unzipped the bag.

"You're almost all packed," Maureen walked in carrying a tray with two steaming mugs. "Thought you might like some company and some tea." Maureen set the tray down on the nightstand.

Charlie wasn't in the mood for company. She preferred to be left alone, but since it was her last day home she didn't say anything to her mom. "Thanks."

For a few seconds neither woman spoke as Charlie continued to pack.

"You look tired. Are you feeling okay?" her mom asked sounding worried. "You haven't been yourself lately."

"Fine. Just a little uptight about the interview in

Virginia. It'd be a big change." Charlie didn't look at her mom as she spoke. The truth was she hadn't slept well since her last conversation with Jake. Every time she lay down her brain would replay their time together, trying to figure out how she'd been so wrong. There must have been hints, but somehow she'd missed them all.

Maureen nodded. "I can't lie. I'm hoping you take the position. But I don't think that's what's been keeping you up." Maureen picked up a pair of shorts, folded them and placed them in Charlie's bag. "Jake called today. He wanted to talk to you. He said he's been trying to get hold of you all week."

Charlie reached for her tea and took a sip. The lemon flavored tea which was her favorite rolled down her throat. "I hope you told him not to call here again."

"He told me what happened and why he's in England."

"And you believed him! Come on, Ma. He probably has a stock pile of excuses that he pulls out when he needs them."

"I don't think so Charlie. He sounded sincere."

She wanted to laugh. Obviously some people never learned to be a good judge of character. "He's no better than my father, Ma. Come on, he just up and left for England to see another woman without a word to me."

Without warning Maureen snatched the t-shirt out of Charlie's hands and tossed it aside. "He's nothing like your father, Charlotte. Your father was manipulative. He wanted to control every aspect of my life. I couldn't go out unless he knew where I was going and who I was with. And he only ever thought of himself." Maureen paused for a moment. "If anything Jake is just the opposite. He worked his butt off here, and he didn't have to. Jake could've let his workers handle everything." Maureen's usual gentle voice took on a hard edge as she spoke. "You're father never would've done that. And do you know that he paid for that ramp at Mr. Quinn's house so he could get in and out while he's in that wheelchair."

Charlie could only stare at her mom. She'd never heard her mom talk about her father in such a negative way. In fact she rarely spoke of him at all.

"I'm not saying you should run off and marry him, but I don't think you're being fair to him either," Maureen said with some calm returning to her voice.

While what her mom said might be true, Charlie wasn't ready to accept any excuses Jake came up with. "I have no desire to end up hurt like you Ma. I think it's best to let things end now."

"Hurt like me? You can't stay out of a relationship because you're afraid to get hurt, Charlie." Her mom's voice had completely returned to its normal gentle tone as she reached for Charlie's hand.

"Come on Ma. You were devastated when my father walked out. No man is worth that."

"It wasn't entirely his fault. He left because I …. cheated on him. He'd gone on a fishing trip. It was the first time we'd been apart since getting married. Even though it only happened once, he somehow found out." Maureen paused for a moment. "I know you're probably wondering how I could do that, but your father and I never should've gotten married."

She could guess what her mom was going to say but still couldn't believe it.

"I was pregnant with Sean when we got married. Our parents pressured us into it. Things were never great between us. I kept hoping he'd change, but it never happened."

Charlie could tell her mom was embarrassed by the conversation. "But you were devastated when he left." She knew she hadn't imagined that.

Maureen nodded. "I did care for him or at least the man he was when we first met, even if he didn't love me. But what scared me the most was being a single mom. I had no job, nothing but a high school diploma and two children. That was the hardest part for me. If it hadn't been for Sean, I'm not sure what I would've done."

She let her mom's words sink in, wondering how she would react in the same situation. "Does Sean know?"

Maureen smiled. "No he just thinks he was born early. I think we should keep it that way."

Nodding Charlie returned her mom's smile. "That still doesn't mean I should give Jake another chance."

"No, but if you do care about him and don't give him one, you'll always wonder. Trust me on that."

Somehow Charlie knew there was another story behind her mom's words, but she didn't think she would get it out of her. At least not now.

Maureen reached for her own tea. "Just consider what I said, Charlie."

"What grand excuse did he give you for being in England? Did the Tower Bridge collapse?" No matter what the excuse, Charlie didn't know if she would believe it anyway.

"You sound as if you've already decided to not believe it." Maureen sighed and shook her head. "You've always been stubborn."

Stubborn? She wasn't stubborn just determined; Charlie thought but kept to herself. She didn't want to get into an argument with her mom on her last day here. "We'll see." For now it was all she would commit to.

"He flew to England because his cousin overdosed and ended up in the ICU. Jake said he had been having problems with drugs and alcohol for a while. The woman you saw in the photo is his cousin's girlfriend. She met Jake at the airport. She asked Jake to come to England."

Charlie remembered him mentioning a cousin who was having substance abuse issues. He'd told her he'd been in England a few months earlier to help him; so it was at least a plausible excuse. Still that didn't make it true.

"It doesn't sound like a story someone would just make up," her mom insisted interrupting Charlie's thoughts. "People don't usually say those kinds of things about their family." Her mom stood.

"That doesn't mean they couldn't."

Maureen rolled her eyes toward the ceiling. "Just think about what I said, Charlie."

***

Man was it good to be home. He'd only been gone ten days but it had felt like a lifetime. He hoped AJ managed to keep things together this time. He didn't want a repeat of his past two visits. Not that he wouldn't do it again if he got the call, but he wasn't sure AJ could survive another setback and he knew for certain AJ would lose Sophia if he did. One relationship had already suffered due to AJ's problems, no reason to make it two.

Jake settled onto the couch and turned on the baseball game. Dylan and Callie were due soon and even though exhaustion threatened to overtake his body, he was looking forward to their visit. He hadn't seen them since the wedding. Another added bonus of their visit was the distraction they would provide. More times than not when he found himself alone he started thinking about Charlie. He still hadn't heard from her and he wasn't sure if another phone call would make a difference. A face-to-face visit might work in his favor with most women but he suspected it'd be a waste of time with Charlie.

He knew she was stubborn, but he hadn't imagined it was this bad. And he wasn't going to beg. Beside, if she was unwilling to at least listen to him what kind of future could they have together?

Even Callie had been willing to hear Dylan out after his disastrous faux pas. And in that case Dylan had been in the wrong.

Forget about it for tonight, he told himself. He couldn't do anything about it at the moment anyway.

***

"How long are you guys staying in Washington?" Jake asked. He, Dylan and Callie were on the deck enjoying dinner.

"The rest of the week. We'll leave on Sunday morning. I'm expected back in the office on Monday," Dylan answered.

Jake couldn't remember the last time he'd seen his half-brother look so relaxed. A type-A workaholic, the guy rarely sat down and put his feet up. At least Dylan had always been that way before meeting Callie. While he was still a workaholic he did at least take time off now to enjoy life and spend time with the woman he loved. Jake envied Dylan in that respect. He wouldn't want to deal with running Sherbrooke Enterprises, but he would like to have someone special in his life. For a short time he'd thought he found her, but apparently he'd been wrong.

"Earth to Jake. Come in Jake."

Callie's teasing voice pulled Jake's mind away from his own thoughts. "Sorry about that. I have a lot on my mind."

Callie studied him for a moment with a quizzical eye but didn't ask him to elaborate. "I asked if you were still seeing the woman you brought to the wedding. Her name was Charlotte right?"

Of all the topics his sister could have brought up, why did she have to choose that one? He wanted to keep his mind off her, not talk about her.

"We broke things off about a week ago." Jake tried to keep the disappointment out of his voice. By the look on Callie's face though, he figured he hadn't succeeded.

His sister reached for her wine and took a sip but Jake could almost see the wheels turning in her head.

"Because of Blair?" she asked.

The paternity suit was just one more thing he didn't want to think about. "No, she handled that okay. She saw a picture of me with AJ's girlfriend and assumed the worst."

Callie opened her mouth to speak, but Dylan interrupted before she got the chance. "When did you see her? Are they here?"

Damn. He told AJ that he wouldn't let anyone else in the family know.

"Last week. I flew to England to see AJ." Jake chose each word carefully. "I just got back. It was a last minute trip."

Dylan's eyebrows knitted together and Jake knew more questions were about to follow.

"Must have been. What prompted that? Weren't you just there a few months ago?"

He should've come up with an excuse just in case family asked about his recent trip, but the thought hadn't crossed his mind. "AJ and Sophia needed some help."

While not the complete truth, it wasn't a lie either.

"Help? What kind of help."

Jake knew Dylan was like a dog with a bone. He wouldn't let a topic go until he was satisfied.

"I can't go into it. But Sophia called and I flew out to help. Some photographer took pictures of us at the airport. Charlie saw them on the Internet and jumped to the wrong conclusion. End of story."

Dylan clapped him on the back. "I hope you gave her more details than that. It's a rather vague excuse."

Jake knew he should be pleased his brother wasn't pressing for more details. "She didn't give me a chance to explain anything. I tried."

Jake didn't miss seeing Callie elbow Dylan in the side in an attempt to shut him up before saying, "Maybe she just needs some time. She's not used to the way the media plays things up. Try calling her in a week."

He knew Callie meant well but it was so obvious she didn't understand anything about male pride. A guy was only going to take no for an answer so many times. After that it would be like begging. He had no intentions of doing that.

"How was Paris?" Jake figured if he got Callie talking about something else she might forget about Charlie for tonight. His ploy worked beautifully. Without mentioning another word about Charlie, his sister launched into a detailed playback of her and Dylan's European honeymoon.

CHAPTER 14

With a groan Charlie kicked her heels off then began to unzip her skirt. After spending more than six hours in the awful shoes her aching feet reminded her why she didn't wear them more often. Today there had been no avoiding it. There was no way she could show up for an interview wearing running sneakers or the clogs she wore when on duty at the hospital.

After slipping on a pair of denim shorts and a t-shirt she put the suit she'd worn in a bag for the dry cleaners and headed toward the kitchen. She'd missed lunch, but she guessed she'd find something yummy in the kitchen. Thanks to Beth there were always freshly baked treats in the kitchen. And judging by the cinnamon scent filling the kitchen, Beth had baked something that morning.

Charlie had one of the rolls half way to her mouth when she saw the magazine pages on the kitchen table. Her roommate was a regular reader of all the popular magazines. She never missed an issue of the weekly publication. By the looks of it her copy of Today had arrived and she'd forgotten to take it with her.

Most of the time Charlie didn't bother with the magazine. Occasionally she would do the crossword puzzle in the back but that was about it. But today it was as if her arm had a mind of its own. It dropped the cinnamon roll and reached for the magazine. Once again on the cover was a close-up shot of Jake. A smile lit up his face and she had to force herself to look away from his sapphire blue eyes. They seemed to almost jump off the page at her.

In an instant her appetite disappeared. For more than two weeks now she'd tried not to think about him, and every time she did, Charlie forced herself to remember the picture she'd seen of him on the internet with his arm around the blonde. Yet every once in awhile a tiny voice in her head whispered what if you are wrong?

Charlie turned the magazine over so Jake's smiling face no longer stared back at her and tossed it onto the counter. She didn't want to know what the magazine had to say about him.

"You okay? You look a little pale."

Charlie's eyes flew open at the sound of her friend's voice. She'd been so distracted that she hadn't heard the door open.

"I saw the cover of your magazine," Charlie nodded toward the counter.

Beth moved toward the cupboards above the counter. "Did you look at the rest of it?"

As her friend turned the other way, Charlie caught the triumphant smile that spread across her face.

"You left it on the table intentionally. Why did you do that?" Beth was one of the few people who knew how much Jake's betrayal hurt her. She didn't consider Beth a cruel thoughtless person so she didn't understand why her friend would leave the magazine behind.

Beth shrugged as she took the seat across the table with the magazine in one hand. "I thought you might be interested in it, but I take it you didn't read the article. He was telling you the truth about Blair. I saw it on Celeb Talk last night and the article confirms that some up-and-coming actor I've never heard of is the father of Blair Peterson's baby."

"So?" Charlie tore off a large chunk of her roll and bit into it in order to give herself something to do. In all the time they'd been friends, Beth had never given her advice unless Charlie asked for it. However she suspected that Beth was about to give her some now and she knew she didn't want to hear it.

"The story he gave your mom could be true too. I don't know if he'd lie about his family like that. Would you?"

"I hear an 'and' coming." Charlie tapped her fingers on the table.

"Since he was telling the truth about this," Beth picked up the magazine. "I'd give him the benefit of the doubt on the other too."

Charlie refused to look at the cover of the magazine. She didn't need to see a picture of Jake. His image was burned into her memory. At least once a day it made a cameo appearance in her thoughts even though she did the best she could to bury it.

"So what if he was, Beth. I don't do long term relationships. You know that. I'm not looking for the ring and the happily-ever-after like you." Charlie recited the words she'd been telling herself and her friends for years, yet somehow they felt hollow today. They lacked any true conviction this time. And deep down in her gut she knew they were not true, at least not anymore. Somehow she'd let her guard down and let Jake sneak his way into her heart.

Charlie tore off another piece of her cinnamon bun. "I'm not interested in having Jake in my life."

Beth raised an eyebrow and pointed her own cinnamon bun in Charlie's direction. "You Charlotte O'Brien are a lousy liar. You've been miserable ever since you got back."

Charlie opened her mouth to protest, but Beth didn't give her the chance.

"You might get away with lying to everyone else but you should at least be honest with yourself."

She hated to admit it, but her friend was right. Despite her words to the contrary she did miss him. But, she didn't know if she was ready to allow someone into her life permanently. That, of course, was assuming he was still interested and felt the same way.

Before she did anything she needed to think. "I'm going for a run. I'll see you later." Charlie dropped the rest of her cinnamon bun onto her plate and stood.

"I'll be here if you want to talk later."

***

Charlie pulled her Jeep into a spot alongside an electric blue Lamborghini that she somehow knew was Jake's and turned off the engine. The coffee she drank on the way over threatened to make a repeat appearance as she sat looking at the building in front of her. It'd been three days since she'd learned the truth about Jake's paternity suit. During those three days her conversation with her mother kept replaying in her head as did memories of Jake's and her time together.

Then the night before, after many internal conversations she'd admitted two things to herself. One that she was afraid to leave the Navy. Sure she loved what she did, but that wasn't the real reason she had been thinking of staying. She was scared to move forward. Afraid of what change might come from leaving her comfort zone, even though in her heart she was ready to start the next phase of her life. Secondly she'd finally admitted to herself that she wanted Jake in her life enough to risk a broken heart. If she didn't at least try she would forever wonder what if.

There was only one huge obstacle in the way now; what if he was no longer interested in her. He hadn't tried to contact her in weeks. Was that a bad sign?

Only one way to find out.

Releasing the death grip she had on the steering wheel,

Charlie opened the car door. A wave of hot humid air hit her, making her already queasy stomach flip in protest.

Before she could stop and reconsider, she slammed the car door closed and started across the parking lot to the building's entrance. A blast of cool air washed over her when she entered the lobby and, as she crossed the marble tiled floor, she thanked God for air-conditioning.

The doors to the elevator on the other side of the lobby were about to close as Charlie approached but the man inside saw her and held the door open for her.

"What floor?" he asked, his fingers hovering over the buttons.

"Six," Charlie answered as she moved toward the left-hand side.

"That's where I'm heading too," the tall well-dressed man replied as the elevator door closed.

She didn't comment. Even on her best day she wasn't into idle chitchat with strangers. Instead she nodded and hoped he took the hint. As the elevator moved up, she tapped her hand against her thigh. Nervous energy coursed through her making it difficult to stand still. To make her unease even worse she could feel the other rider looking at her. He hadn't stopped eying her since she entered.

When the sixth floor lit up and the doors opened she all but bolted out. The Falmouth Foundation occupied the entire sixth floor of the building. With her shoulders back and standing as rigid as she would if she was about to meet a senior officer she walked up to whom she assumed was the receptionist behind a sleek black desk.

"I'm here to see Mr. Sherbrooke," Charlie said in the same no-nonsense voice she used when giving orders at the hospital.

The woman behind the desk pushed the oval glasses up farther on her face. "What time is your appointment?" she asked her fingers poised over the keyboard.

Why hadn't she thought of that before? "I don't have one. But he knows me."

The receptionist moved her hands away from her keyboard. "I'm sorry. He's scheduled for meetings all day. If you want to make an appointment maybe he can see you later this week."

Later in the week? She didn't think she could wait that long. Now that her mind was made up, she needed to execute her plan.

Charlie clenched her fists by her sides. "I only need a few minutes. He must have a little time free today."

"His next appointment is standing behind you."

She'd forgotten that the man from the elevator was behind her.

"I can wait Kimberly. If this is who I think it is, Jake will want to see her. Let Cindy know Dr. O'Brien is here for him."

Charlie whipped her head around toward the man who'd moved to stand next to her. How had he known who she was? Evidently whoever he was, he was more than just a business associate.

The receptionist picked up the phone. "Okay, Mr. Hall."

"Thank you." Charlie bit her tongue to keep herself from asking how he knew who she was.

In response the man extended his hand. "Christopher Hall. Jake told me a lot about you."

She didn't know if that was a good thing or not, but since he was helping her to get what she wanted she decided not to think about it. "I won't be long," she said.

"Take your time."

Just then a slim gray-haired woman came around the corner. "Dr. O'Brien. I'm Cindy Thomas, Mr. Sherbrooke's assistant. Please follow me."

Not a single person glanced her way as Charlie followed the older woman toward the line of office doors on the right-hand side. The assistant stopped at the last closed door in the corner and raised her hand to knock but stopped just before her knuckles made contact.

"You called to speak with Mr. Sherbrooke while he was in England didn't you?"

Charlie nodded curious as to why the woman asked but didn't question her. Any questions would only delay her.

"I wish you had given me your name. Mr. Sherbrooke left instructions to tell you where he'd gone if you called."

Charlie's stomach flipped as guilt mixed with the anxiety already racing through her body.

Before she could think of a response the assistant knocked and entered the office.

"Christopher says to take your time. He went downstairs for coffee," Cindy said. Then she gestured for Charlie to enter and closed the door behind her.

As the door clicked behind her, Jake rose from his spot behind a large meeting table and took a few steps toward her. He was wearing black dress pants and a crisp white shirt. The knot of his red necktie had been loosened and the sleeves of his shirt were rolled up exposing his tanned muscular forearms. For a moment she couldn't do anything but stare at his arms and remember how right it had felt to be held in them. How special and cared for she had felt.

Man, she hoped she hadn't blown things with him. Closing her eyes, Charlie took in a deep breath and then exhaled. It's now or never, she thought as tiny beads of perspiration trickled down her back.

"I know you're busy, but I need to talk to you." Charlie locked her eyes on his face. The barest hint of a beard covered his face reminding her of how he looked first thing in the morning. "And I didn't want to do it over the phone."

So far Jake hadn't said a word but his face did all the talking. Usually his mouth was set in a relaxed friendly smile that made others feel at ease, yet right then it was drawn tight and apprehension lurked in his eyes.

"I'll leave right after I say what I came here to tell you, if you want." Charlie forced her feet to remain still.

Fidgeting would only give away how nervous she was, besides only children fidgeted.

Still in shock at having Charlie show up at his office, Jake nodded toward the chairs around the meeting table. "Do you want to sit?"

Sitting was the last thing he wanted. More than anything he wanted to embrace her and then demand that she explain her behavior. But he didn't do either.

"Not now thanks." Charlie gripped her hands together. "I came to apologize. When I heard you left Virginia and then saw that picture of you with another woman I jumped to conclusions. I shouldn't have done that. I was wrong."

It was on the tip of his tongue to say yeah you were, but he held the words back. Sarcasm wouldn't accomplish anything. "Sophia, AJ's girlfriend, called just after midnight. AJ had just been rushed to the hospital. I didn't have time to call before I flew out. I assumed you would call here when you couldn't get me so I asked Cindy to explain the situation to you when you did. But that didn't happen."

"She told me before I came in."

"When I did call you didn't give me a chance to explain." Jake raked a hand through his hair as the need to know why she'd doubted him increased. Granted he didn't have the greatest reputation, thanks to the media, but he thought she knew him better than that. Until a few weeks ago he'd thought she trusted and cared for him as much as he did her.

Charlie blinked and looked away. "When I heard you were gone and saw the picture it reminded me of ..." Charlie's voice trailed off.

He might not be a psychiatrist but he knew whatever was eating at her ran deep. Without hesitation he took a step closer. With a finger he nudged her face up. The sight of her hazel eyes filled with tears tugged at his heart.

"It reminded me of my father. I was twelve when he just walked out. After I saw the picture I started to think about Blair's baby and it all snowballed."

He knew her parents were divorced but he didn't know the particulars behind it. Though it stung he could understand how she might relate the two.

"You should have trusted me." Resentment leaked into his words and he clenched his teeth from saying anything else he might regret.

A single tear rolled down Charlie's face. Jake couldn't stop himself from wiping it away.

"You're right, but I kept telling myself we were a temporary fling. Nothing serious so it didn't matter how things ended."

Charlie wrapped her arms around herself and Jake suspected there was more to her story.

"My mom was devastated when my dad left. I decided that I never wanted to end up like her. I figured skipping the whole love thing was better. I've always kept relationships strictly fun and unemotional. I figured that was safer." A nervous laugh escaped her. "Until you."

In his mind he could imagine what it must have been like for Charlie as a little girl after her father walked out. Anger toward the man he'd never meet welled up inside him.

"I understand if you don't forgive me, but I needed to apologize. I was wrong and I wanted you to know I'm retiring from the Navy. I sent my retirement documents last night."

Charlie took a step back as if to leave and Jake realized he'd been silent for too long, wrapped up in his own thoughts. "Don't go. I get why you reacted the way you did and I shouldn't have assumed you'd get the message from Cindy. In the future we need to communicate better." Even though she didn't answer him, he wrapped both arms around her slim waist and pulled her close to him. He had no intention of letting her walk out of his office.

Charlie's forehead wrinkled in confusion. "Future?"

"I know my reputation sucks and you probably think I've said this to hundreds of women but I love you, Doc." Once the words were out Jake wondered if perhaps he'd said too much. She'd come by looking for forgiveness not necessarily a declaration of love.

"I love you too." Charlie smiled and put her arms around his neck. "And I don't care about your reputation as long as you're mine."

Jake lowered his head toward hers so he could kiss her. "I'm all yours, Doc."

EPILOGUE

A wolf whistle had Charlie turning toward the door.

"You look incredible." Jake closed the door behind him and walked toward her.

He was dressed in a black tuxedo and she thought the same thing about him. "Thanks. Your sister helped me pick out the gown last month."

During the six months they'd been dating she had developed a close relationship with Jake's half-sister Callie. They spoke on the phone often and whenever Callie came to Washington to see her father she always stopped in for a visit. After having to decline several invitations to visit New York because of work, Charlie had finally made it up the month before.

Jake wrapped his arm around her waist and began to leave a trail of kisses down her neck. "What do you say we skip the party downstairs? No one will notice." Jake reached the base of her throat, then began to work his way back up the other side.

As tempting an offer as it was, Charlie didn't want to miss the New Year's Eve party the Sherbrookes had planned. When she arrived at Cliff House two days earlier the place had already been a buzz of activity with preparations. According to Jake's mother, the Sherbrookes had been throwing a New Year's Eve ball at the mansion since 1900, and it was attended by everyone from top government officials and multimillionaires to A-list celebrities. Every time Charlie thought about that fact she almost had to pinch herself.

Actually she'd been doing a lot of that during the past six months with Jake. Not that she was complaining. She was in love with an incredible man who loved her and she had a fantastic new position at Memorial Hospital. Life couldn't get much better.

"What do you say? Should we let everyone celebrate without us?"

Charlie pulled his arms away from her waist. With him so close she was about ready to give in. "I have a better idea. Let's go down for a little bit then come back up here for our own midnight celebration."

Jake sighed and shrugged his shoulders. "If that is what you *really* want."

She almost laughed at his expression. He looked as if she had just taken away his favorite toy.

"But if we're going down there you're going to need some more jewelry. Everyone down there is going to look as if they just stepped out of Tiffany's."

Other than the diamond stud earrings she had on, Charlie didn't have any jewelry with her. She figured Jake knew that so she didn't know where he expected her to get more. Before she could ask however, she saw him pull a ring-sized jewelry box from his pocket.

"I think this would be perfect," he said holding the open box up to her.

Nestled inside was the largest sapphire she'd ever seen surrounded by tiny diamonds. She'd never seen anything so exquisite up close. Speechless, she stared at it.

"Well?" he asked.

"I don't know what to say. It's gorgeous."

"Simple. Say yes." He flashed her one of his teasing

lopsided smiles. The very one that sent her heartbeat into overdrive.

"Yes? To what? I didn't hear a question." Charlie still didn't touch the ring.

Jake studied her. "Really? You don't get it?" he asked. Then he reached for her hand and slipped the ring on her finger. "Charlotte O'Brien will you marry me?"

Her entire life she'd told herself marriage was the last thing she wanted, but now she wanted nothing more. "How could I ever say no to you?" Charlie didn't give him a chance to respond. Instead she leaned in to kiss him.

Read on for an excerpt from The Billionaire Princess, book 3.

CHAPTER 1

Outside the window, the runway rapidly approached as the family jet touched down. No matter how many times Sara Sherbrooke traveled by plane it never ceased to amaze her how something so large could take off and land with such ease. As the plane rolled to a stop, she released the death grip she had on the armrests and checked her smartphone for any text messages before tossing it into her Coach bag and then waited for the plane door to open.

"Do you require any assistance, Ms. Sherbrooke?" Michelle, the private flight attendant for the jet, asked.

Sara moved toward the exit. "I'm fine, Michelle. I'll let you and Peter know when I'm ready to leave. When you are both done here go ahead and check into your hotel and enjoy yourselves."

Without waiting for an answer Sara walked down the stairs and out into the warm Hawaiian sun. As always it was a gorgeous day. It didn't seem like Hawaii ever had any other kind. At least every time she'd been here the weather was perfect and today seemed to be no different.

A few feet away Sara spotted the limo her brother Jake arranged and started toward it, her curiosity running rampant since yesterday when she'd received Jake's call

194

insisting she come to Hawaii immediately with no explanation. She'd told him she had responsibilities and couldn't just up and leave without a good reason. All he said in response was to reschedule her meetings and then promised to have someone waiting for her at the airport.

"Once you're seated, I'll put your luggage in the trunk; we can leave once Mr. Hall arrives," the driver said opening the door for Sara.

At the mention of Jake's best friend and former college roommate, Sara's curiosity went into overdrive. Just what was her brother up to anyway?

Climbing into the car, Sara made herself comfortable and waited. The temptation to call Jake lurked in the back of her mind, but knowing her big brother the way she did, it would be pointless. When Jake was ready, he'd tell her what was going on and not a minute sooner.

As Sara sat sipping a bottle of sparkling water, the door opened again. Silently, she watched as Christopher Hall climbed in. If she hadn't seen him countless times on the web, she never would've recognized the man who'd climbed in the limo as her brother's Cal Tech roommate. She recalled meeting the tall skinny kid with shaggy light brown hair and glasses when her family moved Jake into his dorm freshman year. On the few occasions she had seen him back then he'd been dressed in jeans, Converse sneakers and t-shirts with hard-rock bands emblazoned on them. The man seated across from her now seemed to be someone else entirely.

Today his light brown hair was cut fashionably short and there was no sign of the glasses he used to wear. And those were not the only changes she noticed. There was no missing the way his broad shoulders filled out his dress shirt.

For a second Sara sat speechless and stared at the man, as her pulse kicked up a few notches. Before he noticed her staring, Sara regrouped and pasted on her best society smile. "Hi Christopher. Did Jake tell you what is going on?"

Christopher shook his head. "No. He just said to get out here, but I have a guess."

Sara expected him to continue and let her in on his suspicions. Instead he grabbed a soda water for himself. When several minutes passed and he didn't say anything else, she couldn't keep herself from asking her next question, "So, what is your guess?"

Christopher paused with the bottle halfway to his mouth. "My money is on a wedding, but it's just a guess."

"A wedding? No. Charlie and Jake wouldn't do that. Our parents would be furious."

"Like I said it's just a guess, but I know Jake and an out-of-the-blue wedding wouldn't surprise me at all."

Would her brother do that to their parents? Sure a sudden unexpected wedding might be something Jake would talk about, but not something he'd ever go through with. Jake Sherbrooke and Charlotte O'Brien's wedding would be a huge affair much like Dylan and Callie's the year before. Considering the size of the Sherbrooke family and the fact that the American public seemed so fascinated by them, how could it be anything less?

But if not a wedding like Christopher predicted, what other reason could Jake have for asking Christopher and her to Hawaii on such short notice? Other than an impromptu wedding like Christopher suggested nothing else made any sense.

"Have you met Charlie?" Sara asked in an attempt to start a conversation. Over the years they'd had few conversations so Sara figured she could either ask him about his company or the one thing they had in common, her brother.

Christopher returned his water to the holder near the door and Sara's eyes watched the way the muscles in his upper arm flexed and moved. The sight sent her hand toward the air vent, which she redirected toward her face.

"I met her last year at Jake's office and we've all gotten

together several times since. I like her. She seems perfect for him."

"I think so too." Sara reached for more water. "She's definitely the right woman for my brother." She took a sip from the bottle and then asked him about his company.

About twenty minutes after leaving the airport, the limo arrived at The Sherbrooke Resort and Spa, one of Sherbrooke Enterprises's finest hotels in Maui. Upon entering the resort Christopher and Sara crossed the lobby to the private elevator behind the hotel concierge's desk and in silence they rode the elevator up to the penthouse apartment, which occupied the entire 21st floor. When the doors opened they walked directly into the living room.

"Good, you two are here. Everyone else is out on the balcony." Jake crossed the room toward them.

Sara dropped her Coach bag onto a nearby table and embraced her older brother. "Care to tell us what's going on?" Before letting go she dropped a kiss on Jake's cheek.

With a devilish smile Jake moved toward Christopher and slapped him on the back. "Why don't you both come outside and join everyone. Then I'll tell you what's up."

"Who else is here?" Sara fell into step alongside Jake and Christopher.

"Charlie, of course, Maureen, Callie and Dylan." He didn't wait for a response before stepping onto the balcony that ran the entire length of the building.

Immediately, Sara thought of Christopher's remark in the car about a wedding. His guess must be right. What other reason could they have for inviting Charlie's mom?

While Jake walked over to his fiancée, Sara took a seat near Dylan and Callie. They sat on an extra-wide padded lounge chair. Dylan's arm rested across Callie's shoulders and their hands were clasped together. Sara fought hard to suppress an eye roll in their direction. Since meeting Callie, her no-nonsense workaholic half-brother had become quite the romantic.

"So are you going to tell us what's up or should we

guess?" Christopher asked the very question on her mind.

"Charlie and I are getting married tonight."

"You'd better be joking or Mom's going to kill you!" Sara looked from Charlie to Jake waiting for one of them to answer her.

"I'm not joking. Dylan and Callie helped us arrange everything. We getting married tonight at five o'clock."

Even though her brother and his fiancée had been engaged since New Year's Eve they hadn't set a wedding date or to her knowledge even started to make formal plans. She guessed they were in no rush.

"What about Mom and Dad?" Sara glanced around at the other people present. No one but Maureen seemed the least bit surprised by Jake's announcement.

"They don't know. And we want to keep it that way," Jake answered.

"Have you lost your mind?" Sara came to her feet. "You cannot get married without them here, Jake. Mom will never forgive you." She knew her brother liked to do things his own way, but she never thought he'd go this far.

In response Jake gave a slight shrug. "It's not about them. Charlie and I don't want a huge affair like Callie and Dylan. That's not us."

Sara couldn't argue with him on that point. She did find it hard to picture Jake and Charlie having such an elaborate and formal wedding. That didn't mean she couldn't see them having something grander than this. And not to have their parents there felt wrong.

"If Mom knew about this she'd insist on making it a big event and then the media would descend. We don't want that. She'll be angry, but eventually she'll get over it."

The way she saw it, saying their parents would be upset was the understatement of the century. At the same time though, she couldn't disagree with her brother that Elizabeth Sherbrooke would insist on turning the wedding into a grand event for the whole world to see.

"I still think that you're crazy." Sara looked over at

Callie and Dylan who had remained silent so far. "And why didn't you tell me about this Dylan, if you both knew." It hurt to think Jake trusted them with the secret but not her.

"Need to know. He needed me to help arrange things. Otherwise he wouldn't have told us either," Dylan answered. "We didn't say anything because we figured the less that people knew, the less likely someone would slip. And it's not like it's been planned for long. We finalized things about three weeks ago."

Dylan's answer made her feel a little better, but not much. She knew how to keep a secret. Their plans would've been just as safe with her. "When do you plan to tell Mom and Dad? I might make plans to be out of the country when you do."

Jake laughed. "I'll warn you before I do. But since they are leaving the country tomorrow it'll be a while."

Christopher watched the exchange between his best friend and the other guests. Jake's announcement hadn't surprised him in the least. Actually, he'd expected something like this since Jake had told him about the engagement. An impromptu wedding near the beach fit the couple in question perfectly. But, judging by their expressions, Charlie's mom and Jake's sister hadn't expected anything like this.

As Sara and Jake discussed their parents, Christopher tuned out the words and watched the emotions on Sara's face, unable to tear his eyes from her. No one could deny that she was an amazingly beautiful woman.

He'd thought the same thing the first time he'd met her his freshman year at Cal Tech. She'd accompanied her parents when Jake moved in, and when she walked into their dorm room, he thought he was seeing a living angel. Even at sixteen, she'd taken his breath away. Not that she noticed him though. At eighteen he'd been tall and lanky, and his personal grooming had ranked low on his priority list. Thanks to the gym and Jake's help, his appearance had drastically changed in the years since they first met. Today no one would recognize him as the geek from Wisconsin and not just because of the changes to his outward appearance.

Sara had changed as well. She'd gone from a beautiful sixteen year old to a gorgeous woman. Though being his best friend's sister meant she was off limits to him. Still, that didn't mean he couldn't admire her from afar. He suspected few men could be in her presence without drooling all over themselves.

"I doubt this surprises you."

Jake's voice broke into Christopher's thoughts and he found himself grateful that his dark sunglasses concealed his eyes. "Not at all. I just thought you'd do it sooner. I told Sara on the ride here I thought we were going to a wedding."

"And she disagreed. What was her theory?" Jake asked with a hint of laughter in his voice.

"She didn't have one or if she did she kept it to herself." Christopher let his eyes travel back to Sara. "But this suits the two of you."

"Thanks for coming." Jake slapped him on the back. "It means a lot to me."

"Hey, I figured if my guess was right I couldn't miss seeing Prince Charming himself get married," Christopher answered, making reference to the title the media had given Jake years before. "Besides, when my sisters hear that you got married they are going to want all the details."

Jake opened his mouth to speak, but Christopher beat him to it. "Don't worry I won't tell them anything until it goes public. If I told them, it would be all over the Internet in an hour."

Jake nodded his appreciation. "I don't think you've meet Maureen. I'll introduce you."

Christopher glanced over at the older woman who was now in a conversation with Charlie and Sara. In silence he and Jake crossed the rooftop to where the three women stood.

"Maureen, I'd like you to meet Christopher Hall," Jake said interrupting.

A wide friendly smile crossed Maureen's face. "You must be Jake's college roommate Charlie told me about. It's nice to meet you." Maureen extended her hand.

"Nice to meet you too. Jake tells me you make the best apple pie he's ever tasted." Christopher extended his hand toward the older woman.

Christopher and the others remained outside. After lunch Christopher retreated to his own bedroom. In addition to having a private elevator, the penthouse apartment had a full kitchen, living room, five bedrooms, and access to a private rooftop pool. During lunch he'd received several text messages from work and he wanted to handle them before the ceremony began.

A few hours later Sara stood between Christopher and Maureen, as Judge Fallon began the wedding ceremony on the deserted beach just feet away from the rolling waves. Sara had to admit the setting of the ceremony fit her brother and Charlie to a T. They both adored the ocean and spent as much time as possible out on Jake's sailboat. The entire feel of the ceremony, in fact, fit the couple. It was low key and informal. There was no over-the-top wedding gown or a tux with tails. And while the ceremony fit the couple beautifully it was far from what she dreamed of having some day, assuming that day ever came. With each failed relationship, Sara began to doubt more and more that she'd ever find the right man. So far she'd managed to find herself attracted to men who only saw her last name—a name with the right business and political connections.

Without intending to, Sara sighed, drawing Christopher's attention. For a moment his dark chocolate brown eyes studied her face and her heartbeat sped up.

After a second or two he looked away, and Sara's heartbeat returned to normal.

Did her brothers know how lucky they both were? They'd both found their perfect matches and neither woman expected anything in return. Although she'd never told Callie or Charlie, she admired them for that. They were both able to see her brothers for the men they were on the inside. Not many people seemed able to do that. At least not many of the ones she'd met.

In front of her, Jake pulled Charlie into his arms and kissed her, signaling the end of the short civil ceremony. Next to her Charlie's mom wept. Without a second thought, Sara wrapped an arm around the older woman's shoulder.

"Are you okay?" she asked, wishing she had a few tissues on hand.

Maureen nodded and wiped at the tears sliding down her cheek. "I just can't believe my baby girl is married. I'll be fine. Go on and join the others." Maureen patted her on the arm and motioned to the others with her head.

Sara hesitated for a second but then moved forward to join the others as they congratulated the happy couple. She listened as both Callie and Dylan welcomed Charlie to the family and then turned to Jake. As children, with only a two-year difference between them, they'd always been close. They had grown apart a bit through the years, since they'd both been sent off to different boarding schools. Yet she still considered him one of her closest friends, the one person she could trust no matter what. So before anyone else could approach him, she moved in and hugged him.

"Congratulations," she said before dropping a kiss on his cheek. "But I still think you're nuts for not inviting Mom and Dad." She couldn't stop herself from adding the last part.

"I'll deal with them later. Besides now they can make an even bigger deal of your wedding when the time comes."

Sara merely shook her head in response. Her brother never cared what their parents thought. Sometimes she envied him for that. "That's more like *if* rather than *when*, Jake." She tried to hide the sarcasm from her voice.

"You're wrong. You'll see. I promise," he said in his annoying big-brother-knows-all tone.

"I'm not going to argue with you on your wedding day." She gave him another hug and moved away before he could offer anymore brotherly wisdom, something he loved to do. He insisted it was his job as her older brother, but she suspected it had more to do with wanting to annoy her.

Whatever the reason, she really didn't want to discuss that particular topic any further. It'd only put her in a bad mood, and she didn't want to ruin the day for her brother and Charlie. Instead she moved toward the bride to congratulate her.

Although Jake and Charlie had been together for almost a year now, Sara didn't know her that well. Charlie and Jake lived in Virginia, while she lived in DC, which should've made visiting easy. But, Charlie was a doctor, and her schedule didn't fit well with Sara's hectic schedule on the Hill.

"Congratulations, Charlie. You look gorgeous." Sara stepped in front of Charlie and hugged her. Today Charlie wore a simple but elegant white gown that ended just above the knee. Her red hair was pulled up with a simple silver comb holding it in place. A simple white gold necklace with an emerald pendant hung around her neck and matching emerald earrings hung from her ears.

Charlie's face beamed with happiness as Sara pulled back. "Thank you. I'm glad you came. Jake was worried you wouldn't make it on such short notice."

"I wouldn't have missed this for the world." Even if she'd been on the other side of the planet, she would've found a way to get to Hawaii when Jake asked her. "Are you two going on a honeymoon?"

"We're spending a few days here, but then I need to get back. In the fall we're going to Scotland and England."

Both were beautiful countries she'd visited many times, but neither were places she'd pick for a honeymoon. "You're going to keep working at the hospital?" Charlie had retired from the Navy and taken a position at a hospital in Virginia the previous fall.

"I love it there, so I see no reason to leave."

Sara mentally nodded in approval. She already knew that Charlie loved her brother and not his money or powerful family name, still Charlie's decision to stay at the hospital further reassured her.

If only she could find a man who'd look past all that too. It seemed as if every man she dated saw her as a dollar sign rather than a flesh-and-blood woman. Perhaps men weren't capable of seeing beyond money and power. After all, the only two people she knew who truly didn't seem to care about those things were Charlie and Callie. Neither had been drawn to their spouses because of material goods. Maybe only women could look beyond what someone had and see the real person, though both of her brothers had dated their share of gold diggers before meeting their spouses.

While Sara pondered the differences between men and women, Charlie told her about why they'd chosen Scotland and England for a honeymoon rather than somewhere more exotic. As she did, the skin on the back of Sara's neck tingled. At first she dismissed the sensation. When it didn't go away she shot a quick glance over Charlie's shoulder, but it revealed nothing out of the ordinary. A large portion of the beach had been closed off to other guests, and any people on the beach were much further down. So far down in fact, she doubted they would be able to tell who had just gotten married.

Still the feeling remained.

Automatically, Sara nodded in response to Charlie's

words as she looked over toward her brother, her eyes locking with Christopher's. For a second or two their eyes stayed connected, his expression unreadable.

What did he see when he looked at her? Did he see the daddy's-little-princess that many of Jake's other friends imagined her to be? Did he see her as some political pawn like her last boyfriend? Breaking contact, she focused back on Charlie and their conversation.

Since she first met Charlie at Dylan and Callie's wedding the year before, she'd tried not to make the same mistakes with her that she'd made with Callie when they'd first met.

"Your brother couldn't come too?" Sara asked. She knew Charlie had an older brother although she'd never met him.

"We invited him but the Victorian Rose expected guests this weekend. He didn't want to cancel those reservations. Jake offered to compensate him for the loss, but Sean insisted canceling at the last minute would be bad for business."

Sara nodded, a negative review on a website somewhere could ruin a small bed and breakfast.

"Ma will tell him all about the wedding when she gets home, and we're visiting them in two weeks."

End of excerpt.

42888798R00119

Made in the USA
San Bernardino, CA
10 December 2016